The
IMAGINARY

A. F. HARROLD

The
IMAGINARY

Illustrated by EMILY GRAVETT

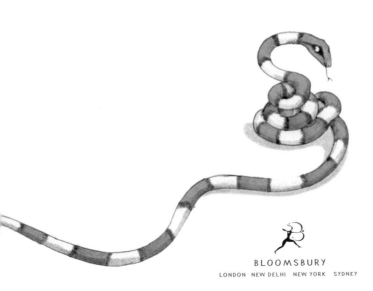

BLOOMSBURY
LONDON NEW DELHI NEW YORK SYDNEY

Bloomsbury Publishing, London, New Delhi, New York and Sydney

First published in Great Britain in October 2014 by Bloomsbury Publishing Plc
50 Bedford Square, London WC1B 3DP

www.bloomsbury.com

Bloomsbury is a registered trademark of Bloomsbury Publishing Plc

Text copyright © A. F. Harrold 2014
Illustrations copyright © Emily Gravett 2014

A CIP catalogue record for this book is available from the British Library

HB ISBN 978 1 4088 5246 0
1 3 5 7 9 10 8 6 4 2

Export PB ISBN 978 1 4088 5727 4
1 3 5 7 9 10 8 6 4 2

Printed in China by C&C Offset Printing Co Ltd,
Shenzhen, Guangdong

CONTENTS

REMEMBER

Remember me when I am gone away,
Gone far away into the silent land;
When you can no more hold me by the hand,
Nor I half turn to go, yet turning stay.
Remember me when no more day by day
You tell me of the future that you planned:
Only remember me; you understand
It will be too late to counsel then or pray.
Yet if you should forget me for a while
And afterwards remember, do not grieve:
For if the darkness and corruption leave
A vestige of the thoughts that once I had,
Better by far you should forget and smile
Than that you remember and be sad.

Christina Rossetti

INTRODUCTION

Amanda was dead.

The words were like a hole through his chest, like a well he was falling down.

How could it be?

Amanda, dead?

But he'd seen her with his own eyes. She hadn't been breathing. She was dead.

Rudger felt sick. Felt lost. Felt like the world had fallen away from him.

He leant on his knees in the park, looking round at the grass and the trees. He could hear birds singing. A squirrel bounced across the path and onto the grass, ignoring him.

How could this all be so green? How could it all be so alive when Amanda was dead?

It was an awful question with an awful answer: one girl's death mattered so little to the rest of the world. It might break him, might destroy her mother, but the park and the town and the world would all go on unchanged.

But Rudger loved the changes, loved how, when Amanda came into a room, it came alive, her imagination colouring it, filling out the details, turning a lampshade to an exotic tree, a filing cabinet to a chest of stolen pirate treasure, a sleeping cat to a ticking time bomb. Her mind was sparky, she made the world sparkle, and Rudger had shared in it. But now…

He looked around at the park. It was the sort of place Amanda would have dreamt into being a whole new world, but no matter how hard he looked, the park stayed stubbornly parkish. He didn't have enough imagination.

In fact, he thought, he didn't even have enough imagination to imagine himself.

He could see the faint outlines of trees through his hands. He was fading. Without Amanda to think of him, to remember him, to make him real, he was slipping away.

Rudger was being forgotten.

He felt sleepy, and sleepier.

What would it be like to fade away? To vanish entirely?

Time would tell, he thought, soon enough, time would tell.

Birds sang him lullabies.

The cool sun shone. He was asleep.

And then a quiet, clear voice said, 'I can see you.'

And Rudger opened his eyes.

ONE

That evening Amanda Shuffleup opened her wardrobe door and hung her coat up on a boy.

She shut the door and sat down on her bed.

She hadn't taken her shoes off before running upstairs and her feet were wet. It wasn't just her feet, either. Her socks and shoes were soaked through too. Her shoes, and the laces.

The knots were cold and damp and hard and refused to come undone. She picked at them with her fingers, but that just hurt her nails. It felt like *they'd* pop off before the knot loosened.

If the laces never came undone, she thought, she'd never get her shoes off. And that meant she'd go through life with wet feet. Not only that, but wearing the same shoes forever. Amanda was the sort of girl (as she'd happily tell you) who *liked* wearing dirty old trainers (because they're comfy and it doesn't matter if they get dirty because they're already dirty), but even she could imagine a day, one day, when she might want to wear *different* shoes.

And also, she thought, what if her feet wanted to grow? At school Miss Short had shown them a bonsai tree. It was an oak tree the size of a dandelion, kept that way by growing it in a small pot.

If she couldn't get her shoes off she'd be stuck girl-size for the rest of her life, just like the tiny root-trapped tree. That was all right today, but in ten years' time, being the size she was now might be less of a good thing. It might, to be frank, be rubbish.

That made it more important than ever to get these shoes off.

Amanda picked urgently at the sodden knot and still nothing budged.

So, after a moment, she stopped. Looked sideways at her feet. Pondered. Hummed. Tutted. Hummed again.

Then, quick as a cat, she ran to her dressing table, pulled open several drawers and rummaged through them, spilling stuff on the floor until she held aloft the object of her search.

'Aha!' she said out loud, feeling like a princess who's just found a dragon tied to a tree and has pulled from her rucksack the exact thing she needs to set it free (a sword, say, or a book about rescuing dragons).

Sitting back down on the edge of the bed, she lifted a foot into her lap, pulled the knot up, slid the blade of the scissors between the taut lace and the tongue of the shoe, and, with a simple and satisfying *snik*, cut it in two.

With the end in sight she quickly tugged at the lace, loosening it all the way down, and pulled the shoe off, chucking it, and her sock, into a corner of the room.

She wriggled her damp toes in freedom.

A moment later she repeated the operation on the other shoe and threw it into the same corner.

Amanda shuffled backwards on the bed. Her feet were pale and clammy and she blew warm air on them and patted them dry with the duvet.

She, Amanda Shuffleup, was a genius. This much was clear. Who else, she wondered, would have found so simple a solution so quickly? If Vincent or Julia had come home with wet shoes (these were friends of hers from school), they'd still have wet shoes on now, and their feet would be *really* cold. So cold, they'd probably have caught pneumonia.

That would never have happened, though, because Vincent and Julia were the sort of kids who didn't spend their Saturday afternoons out in the rain splashing through the biggest puddles they could find. But that just went to show.

'Amanda!' a voice called from the bottom of the stairs.

'What?' Amanda shouted back.

'Have you been treading mud in the carpet again?'

'No.'

'Why's there mud on the carpet, then?'

'It weren't me, Mum,' Amanda shouted, sliding off her bed and onto her feet.

There were footsteps coming up the stairs.

She picked up the wet shoes. Actually, they were a *little* bit muddy, she thought. Sort of. If you looked really hard.

She stood there for a moment, the shoes dangling from her fingertips. If her mum came in and found her holding them like that, and saw the mud on their soles, then she'd *leap to a conclusion*. Amanda had to get rid of the shoes, and quick.

Opening the window and chucking them out would take too long. She could throw them under the bed, except her bed was the sort of bed that didn't have an *under* underneath it, just big drawers, and they were already cram-packed with important junk.

There was only one thing to do.

She pulled open the door to her wardrobe and tossed them in there.

They hit the boy who was still holding her coat. He said, 'Oof,' as the shoes bounced off his stomach and fell to the carpet.

Amanda was just about to tell him off for dropping them when her bedroom door burst open.

'Amanda Primrose Shuffleup,' her mother said in that annoying way mothers have. (They seem to think that if they can remember all your names you'll somehow feel more thoroughly told off. Since, however, they probably named you in the first place, it's never really that impressive.) 'What have I told you about taking your shoes off in the hallway *before* coming upstairs?'

For a moment Amanda didn't say anything. She was thinking fast, but confusion was winning.

There were two doorways. One led out to the landing and was filled up by her mum. The other, that of the wardrobe, framed a boy she'd never seen before. He looked about her own

9

age, held her dripping raincoat, and was smiling nervously at her.

This was a little odd, but so long as her mum didn't bring the strange boy up, Amanda decided, she wouldn't mention him either.

'What have you got to say for yourself?'

'There was knots,' Amanda said, pointing at the filthy shoes that were lying on their sides in between her and the boy's feet. (His shoes were just like hers, Amanda noticed, except cleaner, as if he'd never jumped in a puddle. *Just my luck,* she thought, *a boy appears in my wardrobe, and he's just another Vincent or Julia—afraid of getting mucky. Hmmph.*)

'Knots?' Her mum rolled the word around her mouth as if trying to decide whether it was a good enough excuse. 'Knots. *Knots?*'

'Exactly. So I had to come up here,' Amanda went on, 'to get the scissors, otherwise I'd be stuck in the shoes forever. And then my feet wouldn't grow and—'

'And what's that?' her mum said sharply, interrupting her just before she began an illuminating lecture about bonsai trees.

Amanda stopped talking and followed the invisible line that ran from the tip of her mother's finger straight into the wardrobe.

If Amanda had been her mum, she reckoned this would have been the first thing she'd have done. No going on about wet shoes or anything, she'd've been all about the boy. Either, she reckoned (thinking as if she were her mum), it meant her daughter had been smuggling friends home without asking first, which was against all the rules of politeness, or it

11

meant the house had a case of burglars. That would be bad news, wouldn't it? After all, if this boy could just break in on a Saturday afternoon, who else might be able to break in some other time? They'd be overrun by burglars before you could turn around, and then where would they be? Robbed, that's where.

'I said, "What's that?"' Her mum was still pointing at the boy in the wardrobe.

Amanda screwed up her face, cocked her head to one side and stared intently at him, as if she were giving it a lot of thought.

'It's not really a "What?", Mum,' she said, tiptoeing through her answer. 'It's more a "Who?", don't you think?'

Her mother strode across the room, snatched the dripping wet coat from the boy's hand, turned and held it up.

'What is *this*?' she said, her back to the wardrobe.

'Oh,' said Amanda. 'That's my coat.'

'And what's it doing in there?'

'Hanging up?' Amanda suggested cautiously.

'But, darling,' her mum said, in a quieter voice. 'It's all wet. Look, it's dripping. Hang it up downstairs by the radiator. I've told you before, don't just stick it in the cupboard. It'll get mouldy. When are you ever going to learn?'

'On Monday at school,' Amanda said.

Her mum sighed, shook her head and lowered the coat.

'I'll take these downstairs too,' she said, stooping to pick up the trainers.

The strange boy in the wardrobe smiled at Amanda over her mum's back.

'It was a good joke,' he said.

'What have you done?' her mother gasped, standing up and waving the shoes. 'You've cut the laces!'

'I told you they had knots,' Amanda said, reasonably.

'But you *cut* the laces?'

'Well…'

'Sometimes I don't believe you, Amanda,' her mother said. 'I simply don't believe you.'

She was walking back to the door now.

'Um, Mum,' Amanda said quietly.

'What?'

'You're dripping on the carpet.'

The coat was indeed dripping dirty drops of water and it *was* exactly the sort of thing Amanda's mum would normally have pointed out to her, but this time she just *harrumphed* grumpily and disappeared downstairs.

Oh well, Amanda thought, *you can't expect to understand grownups all in one go.*

She looked at the boy in the wardrobe and he looked back at her.

'You liked my joke then?' Amanda asked.

'It was quite funny.'

'*Quite?*' she snapped. 'I think it's about the funniest joke I've said all day.'

'Yeah,' said the boy. 'But…'

'"But" what?' Amanda demanded, narrowing her eyes.

The boy looked at her. Scratched the side of his head.

She narrowed her eyes further and leant closer. (She had to lean closer because she'd narrowed her eyes so much that leaning closer was the only way she could still see him.)

The boy narrowed *his* eyes, copying her, and leant forwards too.

They were stood nose to nose, squinting and leaning, when Amanda quickly, nimbly stepped to the side. The boy fell forwards and tumbled to the floor in a heap.

'Oh, that was brilliant,' Amanda gasped between laughs. She was clutching her sides and pointing. 'Absolutely brilliant. You fell over! Very funny. Do you want a wine gum?'

And that was how Amanda Shuffleup first met Rudger. Or, you might say, that was how Rudger first met Amanda Shuffleup, depending on whose story you think you're telling.

Rudger had woken up in Amanda's wardrobe just as she'd slammed the front door.

He'd listened to her thundering up the stairs and stood quietly in the darkness, waiting.

Where he'd been before that, he couldn't remember. If he'd been anywhere, it must have fallen out of his mind when he'd woken up.

Now that he'd found Amanda, though, he had a feeling in the

bottom of his stomach of *rightness*. As if he'd been made for her. As far as he could tell she was his first friend. She was also his only friend, and therefore his best friend.

A week after they first met, Amanda took him to school with her to show him off to Vincent and Julia. They were very polite because they knew Amanda was a bit odd. When she said, 'This is Rudger,' and pointed at him they looked at a bit of empty space nearby and shook its hand, except it didn't have a hand because it was just empty space. But when Amanda said, 'No, not *there*, *here*, stupid,' and pointed to exactly where he was, they laughed and said, 'Sorry,' and tried to shake his hand again. Julia jabbed him in the stomach and Vincent, who was taller, almost poked his eye out.

It was clear to Rudger and Amanda that only she could see him, no one else. Obviously he was Amanda's friend, not to be shared, and Rudger rather liked that feeling.

That was the first and last time he went to school.

TWO

Amanda and Rudger spent the early part of the summer holiday in the garden, mainly. They built a den at the far end, under the thorn bush, and through her eyes he saw the place transformed.

One day the den would be a spaceship landing on far-off alien planets. They'd climb out through the thorns, taking great care not to prick their spacesuits, and walk across the surface of their strange new home in great slow loping bounds, buoyed up by low gravity. They'd marvel at weird rock formations and the extra moons in the sky and chase the strange cat-sized animals that lived on this distant world.

Another day the den would be the gondola of a grand hot-air balloon, setting them down atop a rocky plateau miles above the sticky, steamy South American jungle. They'd dare each other to look over the edge (or, rather, Amanda would dare Rudger to look and then, when he refused to do it, do it herself to prove how easy it was), and chase the strange cat-sized animals who'd been up there for millions of years.

At other times the den would be an igloo and the garden would glitter with ice, or it would be a thick dark nomad's tent and the garden a dusty, parched, hazy desert, or it would be a future-tank trundling endlessly over trackless, cratered, muddy fields.

Wherever they ended up Amanda's mum's cat, Oven, would watch them carefully from the patio, waiting for the moment Amanda would see her. Through Amanda's imagination-tinted eyes, Oven would always play the part of the alien or tiger or dinosaur that needed chasing.

At first Rudger had felt sorry for her, but she always escaped with a rattle of cat flap as soon as Amanda pounced.

Sometimes, he thought, it seemed as though Oven could see him. She'd catch his eye in the middle of washing her shoulder and stare worriedly, her unmoving pink tongue poking out, but then she'd blink, yawn, turn around, lift her leg and begin licking her wide-spread toes as if she'd seen nothing after all. So, who could say?

Well, Rudger thought, upon reflection, Oven could say, but since she was a cat and cats don't speak, he resigned himself to living without knowing.

One day Rudger and Amanda were exploring a complex of caves, deep and dark, that stretched out for unknown miles underneath the stairs. They smelt of damp and bats and dripping water, and Amanda was just complaining that Rudger had forgotten to bring the torch, when the doorbell rang.

As the echo of chiming bells reverberated through the caverns they heard Amanda's mum grumble her way to the front door. She was working in her study and didn't like being disturbed.

'Yes?' she snapped as she pulled the door open.

'Oh, hello,' said a deep voice Amanda didn't recognise. 'I am in your area with a survey. Do you mind if I ask a few questions?'

'What's it about?'

'It's a survey,' the voice replied. There was a long pause as if this were answer enough before it then added, 'about Britain today. And children.'

'I'm not sure,' Amanda's mum said. 'Do you have any identification?'

'Identification?'

'Yes, to say who you are.'

'Who I am? My name is Mr Bunting, ma'am. Like the bird.'

'Bird?'

'Yes, the corn bunting, for example. There are others…'

'Yes, yes,' Mrs Shuffleup agreed. 'Do you have something to prove that?'

'To prove a kinship to the bird?' the man said. 'No. No, nothing like that. Ornithology is not—'

'No,' Amanda's mum interrupted. 'I mean ID? To prove you are who you say you are?'

Mr Bunting gave a little cough, as if he were insulted (but only a tiny bit), before saying, 'Yes, of course. I have a badge, look.'

By now Amanda had crept into the hallway. She left Rudger in the cave-mouth under the stairs so she wouldn't lose her place in the adventure (in much the same way you leave your thumb in a book when someone talks to you). She tiptoed up behind her mother and gave her a hug. Mothers like this sort of thing. From there it was easy for Amanda to be nosy.

Peering round her mum she discovered two people on the doorstep: one a grown man, showing her mother his name badge, and the other a little girl about Amanda's age.

The man was dressed in Bermuda shorts, with a brightly patterned shirt, all clashing colours and dazzle, stretched across his

Mr Bunting

wide round torso like palm trees bending in a tropical breeze. He clutched a clipboard in his hands, had a biro behind one ear, and was completely bald. A pair of dark glasses covered his eyes and a red moustache covered his mouth. It quivered each time he spoke.

The girl, in contrast, was dressed in a dull, dark dress over a white blouse. It was practically school uniform, Amanda thought. Her hair was straight and black and from between its dull falling curtains her eyes shone dimly out. She stood still while the man bobbed and wobbled about. She didn't say anything.

Amanda guessed that the man was her dad and she'd had to go to work with him. She knew that sometimes some of her friends had to do this during the holidays. It didn't look like she was enjoying it.

Then the girl turned and looked at her, straight in the eyes. The suddenness of it made Amanda jump (not that she'd admit it); nevertheless, she managed to squeeze a smile out at the girl. It was good to be friendly, Amanda believed, and the girl looked so miserable it seemed the only kind thing to do. The pale girl smiled a small thin-lipped smile back at her and, as she did so, reached up and gave the man's sleeve a tug.

He stopped talking.

'I'm not really sure I want to answer questions on the doorstep,' Amanda's mum was saying. 'Maybe, if you've got a form you want to leave? Something I can pop in the post? Or… It's just I *am* pretty busy right now.'

She made a typing movement with her hands in the air as if to emphasise the point.

'Oh, no need, ma'am,' the man said with a happy chuckle. 'No need at all. I'm very sorry to have troubled you on this pleasantly weathered afternoon. I will leave you now. Be off, eh?'

He pulled a handkerchief from his pocket and mopped at his brow, before spinning on his heel and walking off up the front path.

When she'd shut the front door Amanda's mum said, 'How odd.'

'What did they want, Mum?'

'He was asking about how many children live here and things like that. Seemed most peculiar to me, darling. That's why I got rid of him so quickly.'

'And she looked so miserable, having to follow him round,' Amanda said, going back up the hallway to where Rudger was waiting.

'*She*, darling?'

'The girl.'

'What girl?'

Amanda looked at her mum with her head on one side.

'Oh, nothing,' she said, waving her hand and sending her back to her work. It was important stuff and Amanda did her best to not get in the way. 'I was talking to Rudger.'

'Rudger,' her mum said indulgently. 'Is he okay? You two been busy today?'

'Yes, we're potholing.'

And then Amanda was back in the caves, feeling her fingertip way through the black, edging round ancient vacuum-cleaner-shaped rock formations and between dim dank dark-dripping stalactites. She told Rudger about what she'd seen.

'And she didn't see the girl?' he asked.

'No.'

'Wasn't she looking?'

'Oh, she was looking all right. She's not stupid, not *really*. Do you know what I reckon, Rudger?'

'Yeah, I think so.'

'That bloke. He had a 'maginary friend, just like I've got you.'

'Well,' said Rudger, 'it's nice to know I'm not alone.'

Some children need their parents to pay them a lot of attention. Some children need constant watching. Their day is somehow wasted if there's no grownup around to witness everything they do. They get bored if they're left on their own for more than five minutes (less, sometimes). They sulk and slump and kick their heels and grumble.

Amanda had never been one of those children. She'd always been quite content off by herself. When she was little she'd spend hours with big bits of paper and boxes of pens and crayons, drawing maps and monsters and planning adventures. She was more than happy to sit on her bed reading books or sailing the ocean. When she went round other children's houses for birthday parties and sleepovers the other children's parents would sometimes phone her mum up and say things like, 'I've just found Amanda sat under the kitchen table. She said her boat had been swallowed by a whale and she was waiting for it to be sick. Um… Would you like to come and collect her?' To which Amanda's mum would say, 'Does she *want* to come home early? Has she broken anything? No? Then I'll be over at six as arranged.'

Because Amanda was so good at entertaining herself, at inventing adventures and exploring made-up stories of her own, her mum, even in the school holidays, could spend most of her time working in her study (sending off e-mails and spreadsheets to Mr and Mrs Shuffleup, Amanda's grandparents, for whose business she did the accounting), or pottering in the kitchen waiting for the kettle to boil while listening to the radio, or laid on the sofa with her feet up (just for ten minutes) with a glass of wine in the middle of the afternoon, and sometimes she'd quite forget (almost) that she even had a daughter.

Which is not to say Mrs Shuffleup was anything other than a good mother or to imply that she *wouldn't* have instantly pressed *Save* on her computer and sat down to read a book with Amanda or played a board game or helped her with her homework or gone to the pictures, had Amanda just asked. Nevertheless, it pleased her that Amanda was the sort of girl who was quite happy to get on with stuff by herself. Perhaps because it made her feel less guilty about spending so much time working in her study.

One Sunday morning, a few weeks after Rudger had made his first appearance, Mrs Shuffleup answered the telephone. She was sat at her desk, looking past the computer screen and out of the window into the garden where Amanda was playing.

At the other end of the phone was her mother, Granny Downbeat, as Amanda called her. They chatted for a while, as adults do, about this and that until Mrs Downbeat asked after her granddaughter.

'Is she around? Does she want to say hello?'

'No, Mum,' Mrs Shuffleup said, 'she's out in the garden playing with Rudger. I don't want to interrupt her.'

'Roger?' her mother asked. 'Is that a new friend?'

'Sort of. He's new, yes, and he's a friend, yes, but, well…'

'What is it?'

'You're going to laugh, Mum. You're going to say I indulge her too much, or that I ignore her too much. One or the other.'

'Don't be silly, love,' her mum said. 'Go on.'

'Rudger's not really real.'

'Not real?'

'No, he's imaginary. Amanda dreamt him up the other week, but they've become inseparable. He has to have a place set at the table and everything. Don't laugh.'

But her mother wasn't laughing. Instead, she sounded wistful. 'Oh, Lizzie, love,' she said. 'Do you remember Fridge?'

'The fridge?' Amanda's mum asked. 'What are you talking about?'

'*Your* old imaginary friend, dear. I think he was a dog, wasn't he? It's a long time ago now, of course, but when you were little you wouldn't go anywhere without him. The cats wouldn't go in the room when he was there. You'd chase them out so that he wouldn't get scared.'

'I don't remember that,' Amanda's mum said, wondering how she'd forgotten something that sounded so memorable.

'Oh dear. You ask your brother next time you speak to him,' her mum said. 'You and Fridge used to drive him potty.'

And after that the conversation moved onto other things, weather and work, artichokes and arthritis, the usual sort of boring grownup subjects.

Once she'd put the phone down Amanda's mum sat at her desk in silence for a few minutes. She looked out of the window at the garden and smiled as she saw Amanda leaping off the bench with blue paint on her face and a stick in her hand, yodelling like some ancient Pictish warrior and scaring poor Oven out of the flowerbed.

The cat flap rattled in the kitchen.

She leant back in her chair and thought of Fridge. Now her mum had reminded her, she found she did remember something. She could *almost* remember what he looked like. Had he been an old sheepdog? Maybe. It had been so long ago, and although she had a sense that she remembered some things (the damp, earthy, musty smell of the dog as he slept under her bed, for instance), most of what had slipped out of her mind as she'd grown up remained lost.

What *was* clear, though, was that inventing a friend hadn't done *her* any harm, and so she wasn't going to worry on Amanda's behalf. While some adults she knew would be on the phone to the child psychologist at the first hint of an imagination in their child (heaven forbid such a terrible thing!), she was more than happy to share a house with Rudger.

If there was an extra place to lay at the dinner table, then so be it. If she had to buy the special strawberry-scented shampoo the imaginary boy preferred, well, that was easy enough. If they had to make sure his seatbelt was done up in the car before they drove anywhere, these were all small prices to pay for a daughter who was happy.

Besides, from everything Amanda had told her about Rudger, he didn't seem like a bad influence. In fact, secretly, she worried a little for *his* sake.

THREE

That evening Amanda's mum was going out. She didn't go out often, but when she did she always managed to find the most annoying babysitter she could to get in Amanda's way.

Amanda was quite old enough to be left on her own without a babysitter. Babysitters were for babies, she'd tell you (the clue is in the name), and she hadn't been a baby for years. Besides she wouldn't be on her own, would she? She'd be with Rudger.

But it happened every time: Amanda would rehearse the arguments, loudly, intelligently, pleadingly, and the babysitter would turn up just the same.

'It's as if,' Amanda said to Rudger, 'she doesn't trust us. I blame you.'

'What?' said Rudger, taking umbrage at the accusation.

'Well, you *did* break that vase of hers throwing the ball round in the dining room that time.'

Rudger's jaw hung open.

'Firstly,' he said, counting on his fingers and wondering if he'd have enough, 'it was a *jug* and not a vase; secondly, it was *you* and not *me* who threw the ball; thirdly, it was an *orange* and not a ball; fourthly, *you* said it was a *hand grenade*, not an orange—'

'And fifthly,' she interrupted, 'I told her it was *you*, Rudger, because you're my shining knight who takes the blame, otherwise she'd have been dead angry with *me* and I wouldn't have been allowed burgers on Friday. Did I say "Thank you"?'

Rudger was confused, but that wasn't unusual. He scratched his elbow.

The doorbell rang.

They ran downstairs to find Amanda's mum opening the front door to a tall teenage girl. She was stood in the rain under a dripping black pop-up umbrella and talking loudly into her mobile phone.

'Yeah, so like I'm at the house now,' she was saying to whoever was listening. 'Gotta go. 'kay? Speak later, yeah? Mwah! Mwah!' She made loud mock kissing noises.

Amanda looked at Rudger and tried not to laugh.

'You've got my number, haven't you?' Amanda's mum was saying. 'I'll be back about ten. Thanks awfully for coming out at such short notice.' She turned to Amanda and said, 'You be on your best behaviour for...oh, sorry, what was your name again?'

'Marigold, but everyone calls me Goldie.'

'Isn't that a dog's name?' said Rudger quietly.

Amanda giggled and her mum said, 'Be nice.'

'It wasn't me,' Amanda said. 'Rudger said something funny, that's all.'

'Oh yes,' her mum said. 'Amanda's got a friend called Rudger, but don't mind him, he's no trouble.'

'There's two of them?' Goldie asked. 'You didn't say there'd be two.'

'Oh no.' Mrs Shuffleup laughed. 'There's no need to worry. Rudger's *imaginary*.' She half-mouthed, half-said the word, but still everyone in the hallway heard it.

'Mum!' Amanda protested. 'He's standing right here. He does have feelings, you know.'

Mrs Shuffleup looked at her daughter for a moment, took in the crossed arms and the frown, and said, 'Sorry, love, I didn't mean to be rude.'

'Well, it's not me you should be apologising to, is it?'

Amanda didn't uncross her arms until her mum looked round and said, 'Sorry, Rudger,' to the thin air nowhere near where Rudger was stood.

'Apology accepted,' said Rudger.

'He says he forgives you,' Amanda said.

After she'd made herself a cup of tea Goldie said, 'So, where's the biscuits?'

The three of them were sitting at the kitchen table. The room was warm and the back door was open. Although rain was falling

hard on the patio, the evening hadn't got cold yet. The air smelt clean, tangy, almost electric. The storm had swept away the close sticky dull afternoon, and although the clouds hung low and dark, and the thunder grumbled overhead, the rain felt good, and the evening felt fresh.

'In the jar,' Amanda said, pointing. 'Mum says we're allowed two each.'

The babysitter pulled the biscuit barrel across the table and lifted the lid.

'Okay, so two for you,' she said, extracting a pair of cookies with her long fingers. 'And two for me.'

She replaced the lid.

'*And* two for Rudger,' Amanda said.

'Rudger?' asked the girl, confused.

Amanda rolled her eyes and said, 'Of course Rudger. Mum *always* lets him have two biscuits too, 'cos he's a growing boy and needs his vitamins.'

Goldie slapped the table and smiled as she remembered, laughing. 'Of course! Your imaginary boyfriend. When I was—'

Whatever Goldie was about to say was forgotten as Amanda spat the nibbled corner of cookie all over the table in shock.

'He's not my *boyfriend*,' she said, sounding utterly outraged at the very idea. 'Ugh, uh, uh.'

She waggled her hands at her mouth as if she could somehow expunge the bad taste through the power of waving.

Rudger sat in his chair and stared at her. He didn't like the suggestion any more than Amanda did, but he wasn't sure all the theatrics were *entirely* necessary.

'Calm down,' he said.

She glared at him, aghast. 'Calm down?' she repeated as if she couldn't believe what she was hearing.

'*Mandy and Roger sitting in a tree,*' Goldie sang between sips of tea. 'K-I-S-S—'

'That's not even his name,' Amanda snapped, turning on the babysitter with a glare.

'Pardon?'

'It's not *Roger*,' she said firmly. 'It's *Rudger*. And I'd be dead before I'd kiss him.'

Goldie stared at Amanda for several long seconds before she put her mug down. She looked like a babysitter getting out of her depth. 'Whatever you say,' she said.

'Hmm.' Amanda huffed and crossed her arms. 'Just so long as you remember that. Rudger is *not* my boyfriend. And you've not given him his two biscuits yet.'

Goldie reached into the biscuit barrel and pulled out two more. She looked at Amanda as if to say, 'Where do I put these?'

Amanda said, 'Anyway, Rudger don't much like biscuits, so I'd best look after them for him.'

She took the cookies and kept them safe. In her stomach.

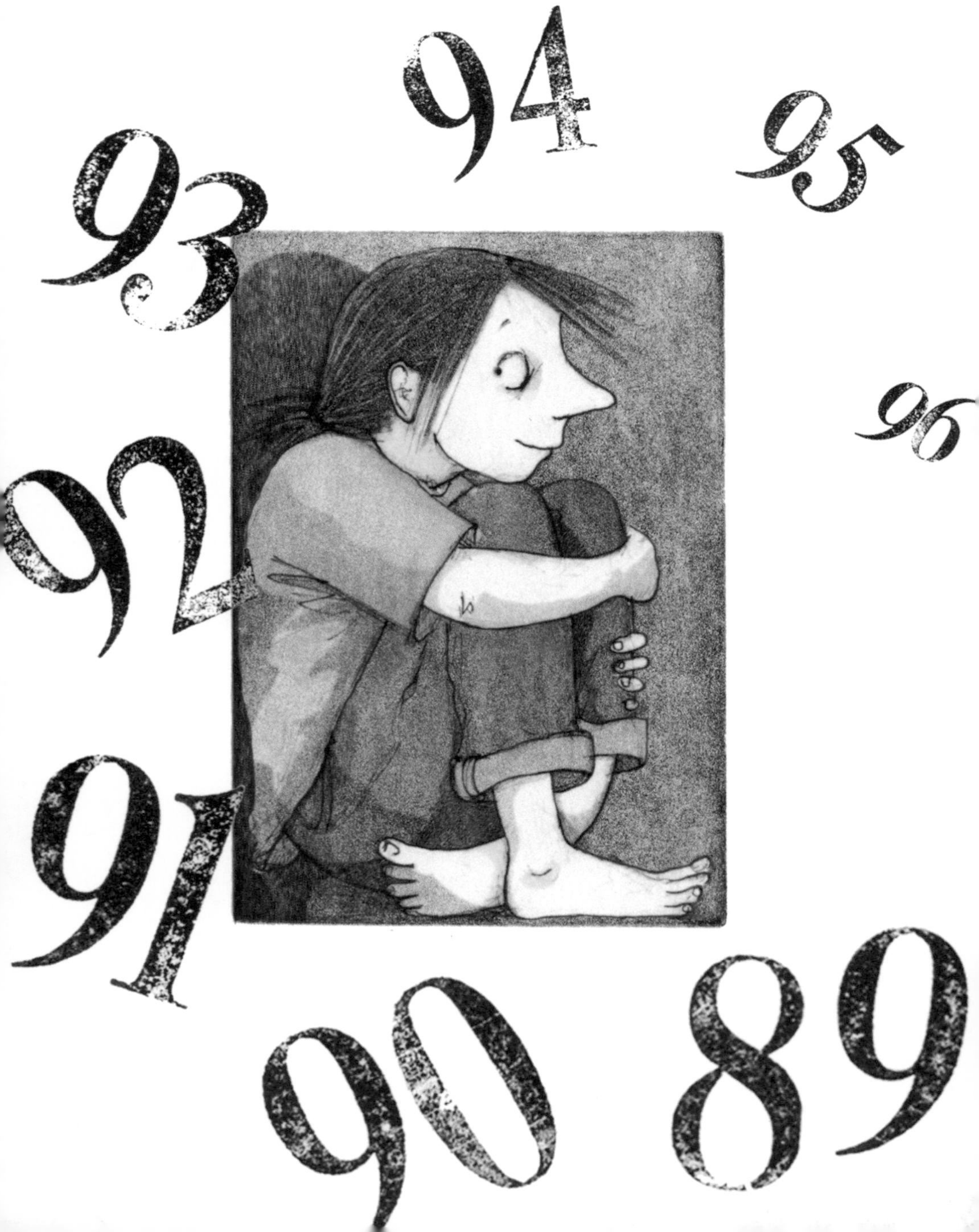
89
90
91
92
93
94
95
96

Ten minutes later Goldie stood in the hallway with her eyes shut. She was counting.

Upstairs Rudger sat in his wardrobe, the same wardrobe he'd appeared in. He knew it was the first place Amanda would've looked for him, but tonight she wasn't the one seeking.

Downstairs Amanda had tiptoed into the study and tucked herself into the space under the desk where her mother's legs normally went. She'd pulled the chair in behind her so she was almost completely hidden from sight. She sat with her knees up under her chin and her back to the wall like a subterranean gargoyle and waited.

'Ninety-eight…ninety-nine…a hundred,' Goldie called from the hallway. 'Coming ready or not!'

Amanda listened to the silence of the babysitter's thinking. She could picture the look on the teenager's face. Should she go upstairs or downstairs? Check the kitchen or the front room? Look under the lampshade or under the table? How to begin the search?

There was a buzz of excitement in Amanda's stomach. She listened to the kitchen cupboards being opened and closed one after another, then the under-the-stairs cupboard door gave its usual creak. Goldie was certainly being thorough. This was good.

After a moment's quiet Amanda heard the babysitter's footsteps come closer. Through the legs of her mum's chair she saw the silhouette of the girl in the doorway. Goldie reached out, flicked on the study light.

Amanda resisted the urge to wriggle back further under the desk. Making a noise at this moment would be disastrous. *Keep still,* she told herself, *keep quiet.*

Goldie looked around at the bookcases and then pulled open the top drawer of Mrs Shuffleup's filing cabinet. Amanda wasn't in there. She took a step into the middle of the room.

Amanda could see her legs, and watched her turning in a slow circle. She thought about the study. There weren't any cupboards to hide in, there wasn't a laundry basket or a wing-backed armchair for a girl to crouch behind. In fact, she realised with a sinking feeling, the only hiding place in the room was the place where she was hiding. Even Goldie was bound to work it out any moment.

And then the doorbell rang.

And Goldie went to answer the front door.

There was a boom of thunder that rattled the windows and Amanda shifted underneath the desk. Her left leg had begun to go to sleep. This was a good opportunity to get comfortable, while the babysitter was distracted.

'I'm sorry to bother you, young lady,' said a man's voice from the hallway, 'but my car has broken down…there. It's a dreadful weathered evening tonight…my portable telephone is out of… be so kind as to let me borrow your telephone to call for…'

'Um,' said Goldie, the uncertainty in her voice obvious. 'Well, it's not my house. Mrs Shuffleup, she's out right now. I'm just the babysitter. I don't know if I…'

'Oh, I understand. Really I…been left in charge of an…and you feel troubled by a stranger knocking. But…will only take a moment. Really… Do be my saviour, young ma'am. What harm…'

Amanda didn't hear everything, because the rain was thudding loudly against the study window now, but she had the oddest feeling she recognised the voice. It wasn't a voice she knew, she was sure it wasn't one of her mum's friends and it wasn't one of the neighbours, but…

'Well,' Goldie was saying. 'It's not my house, I…'

'Of course, of course, I understand. No harm… I see the light's on next door. I'll try there. Good evening.'

'Yeah, 'kay. Night.'

The front door shut and the sound of the rain on the front path was hushed. Still, that voice was working its way round the inside of Amanda's brain. She couldn't *quite* place it. It was most annoying, but the man was gone now, so, she said to herself, never mind.

And then the lights went out.

Two minutes earlier, Rudger had crept out of the wardrobe. From Amanda's bedroom window you got a good view of the front garden. He climbed carefully, quietly up on to her bed and pressed his face against the cold glass.

It was amazing how dark it had got out there. It was as if night had fallen early, but it was just a covering of huge black clouds that were dumping their warm damp contents over the town.

He peered down. He could see the path and the light from the hallway spilling out of the house. There was a person-shaped shadow in the middle of it, but the caller himself was out of sight, tucked under cover by the front door. Rudger would need to open the window and lean out to be able to see who it was, but he didn't feel *that* inquisitive, especially not when a sudden gust of wind flung a vicious squall of rain right against the pane.

Rudger jumped with fright, bouncing on the bed. He stood there wobbling for a moment before he heard the front door bang shut downstairs.

He leant forward once again. Water was pouring down the window, but he could just make out the shape of someone walking back up the path. It was a big man, Rudger could see that much. He was underneath an umbrella and appeared to be wearing shorts.

When he reached the pavement he turned to face the house and just stood there, as if he were waiting for something.

That's odd, Rudger thought.

And then the lights went out.

Back downstairs Goldie was shouting in the dark hallway. 'Hey, 'Manda! Don't panic. It's just a power cut. Nothing to worry about. Where are you?'

Power cut or no power cut, Amanda wasn't going to be tricked into giving away her hiding place. She sat quietly where she was and didn't say a thing.

'Let me get my phone out. Use it like a torch,' Goldie said.

Amanda heard a *thunk* as something fell to the floor, presumably the mobile in question. The babysitter obviously had butterfingers. Amanda pretended not to hear the bad language that accompanied them.

'Oh, where are you?' Goldie muttered frustratedly.

Amanda couldn't see round corners, or in the dark, but she could picture the scene as Goldie scrabbled around on her knees in the hall searching. Maybe she *should* disentangle herself from under the desk, and go and help her look. But then she'd lose the game and she didn't like losing. She decided to stay still and a second later was glad that she had.

A flash of lightning lit the study and, through the wooden legs of the chair, she saw, illuminated in the split-second snap of light, a pair of thin pale human legs stood in the middle of the room.

Then it was dark again.

Amanda gasped at the unexpected sight and clapped her hand over her mouth. Her brain buzzed. *Keep quiet, keep still*, it whispered.

The rain lashed against the windows and Goldie was still shuffling around in the hall. (Amanda heard her bang into the little table on which the post was put.)

She waited for the next rumble of thunder and crack of lightning with bated breath. She dared not move. The one thing she knew from the glimpse she'd got was that they *weren't legs that she knew*. They weren't Goldie's, they weren't Rudger's, they weren't the cat's and they weren't her own. And there was no one else in the house. Or rather, there was *supposed to be* no one else in the house.

Of all the legs she'd considered, they looked most like hers. White socks under a black dress and black buckled girls' shoes. Not that Amanda wore buckled shoes, except for school. She wasn't wearing *any* shoes now.

'Amanda! Come and help me look for my phone. I think it's fallen underneath something. Do you know where there's a torch?'

A startling flash of lightning lit the room at the same time as the house was shaken by a great cracking boom of thunder, the biggest yet, directly overhead.

Amanda was staring exactly where she thought the legs had been, but this time she didn't see the girl's legs. They'd vanished.

Instead, between the legs of the chair hung a face. An ashen girl's face, curtained on either side by long straight black hair. It was a sad face, grim and small-mouthed, and it was looking straight at her.

And the room was in darkness again.

Amanda did something she hadn't expected to do, something quite out of character: she screamed. Without thinking she kicked out at the chair, and at the place the girl had been crawling.

It was ridiculous, she thought later on, to scream like that—to scream like a girl—when all she'd seen was a face lit up in the dark, and maybe not even that. It had flashed before her so fast, so briefly, could she even be sure she'd seen a face at all? (The answer to that, upon a moment's reflection, was 'Yes'.)

Within seconds Goldie had run into the study, knocking over the wastepaper basket and swearing again. She had her phone held out in front of her, the screen illuminating the room with a hazy blue glow.

And there was no one there.

Goldie pulled the chair away from the desk and put a hand out to help Amanda to her feet.

They were without any doubt the only two people in the room. Amanda looked around and Goldie pointed her phone in all the corners.

'There was a girl here,' Amanda said, breathing heavily.

'Well, there's no one here now,' Goldie replied, putting a hand on Amanda's shoulder. 'You probably imagined it. It's the dark, the *unexpected* dark. Power cuts are spooky like that. There, there.' She patted Amanda's head, which at any other time would have infuriated her. Right now she hardly noticed it, she was too busy thinking.

Amanda knew she hadn't imagined it (had she?), but she didn't know what else to say. Her brain was ticking through the house, wondering where the girl might have got to, and in that moment she thought of Rudger.

Upstairs Rudger was still in the bedroom. He couldn't see in the dark any better than a real boy.

When he heard Amanda's scream he ran for the doorway. It stood as a darker rectangle in the dark grey of the room's wall. Before he reached it, a third burst of lightning flashed its stark glare through the windows and he saw her, stood there.

The girl. The one with the long straight black hair, the dark dress, the white socks and the half-hidden deep sad eyes.

He recognised her from Amanda's description. She was the imaginary friend of the man who'd come to do a survey that afternoon. There was no question, no doubt about it.

Even if Amanda hadn't told him what she was, Rudger would've known. He couldn't say how, couldn't say what gave the game away, what tipped the last clue into his hands, but he could tell she wasn't *real*. Maybe it just takes one to know one, as the old saying says.

But it was only a flash of lightning and as soon as he saw her, as soon as he knew who she was, the darkness returned and he found himself flying backwards.

She must've run at him and now her cold hands were gripping his T-shirt and she was pushing him backwards into the bedroom.

She was stronger than she looked. Stronger even than Amanda was. (Sometimes an argument with Amanda turned into a wrestling match and Rudger always lost, partly because she was pretty strong for a girl and partly because she cheated.)

His foot caught on the edge of a rug and they tumbled backwards, the girl on top of him. Her hair fell into his face like spiders' webs and he tried to blow it away.

'Get off,' he gasped between puffs. 'Let go of me.'

She got off him, but she didn't let go.

She picked herself up and clambered to her feet, all in the dark, and pulled him toward the window. His T-shirt dragged half off as he, and the rug he'd fallen on, slid across the floor.

Another lightning bolt split the sky and looking up he saw her pale arms and that straight black hair. He didn't see her face (it was turned away) but he felt something dreadfully wrong about her.

It wasn't just that she'd attacked him, knocked him over, and was dragging him away. These things, of course, *were* wrong and unexpected, but on top of all that, on top of the frightening, weird turn this evening had taken, there was something else. He felt it in his heart, the way it was beating slower rather than faster, a tingle down his spine like a dull trickle of boredom. This girl was not *right*.

She heaved him onto Amanda's bed and finally let go. He could see her now, in front of the window, lit by the orange glow of a street light. She was touching the lock of the window handle with her fingertip.

She hissed and there was a *click* and then she was turning the handle and a windy spray of rainwater whipped into the bedroom.

'Help!' he shouted, rolling himself off the bed. 'Amanda!'

And as he shouted a different sort of light swung across the window, circling round the bedroom wall, and he heard the revving of a car, and then silence as the engine was switched off.

Just the rain pattering outside.

The girl hissed again as they heard the clunk of a car door.

She turned to look at him. Silhouetted as she was in the window he couldn't see her eyes, but he felt them burning icily into him. His knees wobbled.

There was a buzz in the air, a flicker from somewhere behind him and Rudger heard the noise of a key turning in the front door.

Lights came on all over the house: in the hallway, in the study, in the kitchen, on the landing.

A shaft of bright light poured into Amanda's bedroom. A lopsided rectangle of light that ran from the door right across the carpet and up onto the bed.

Rudger looked round, just for a moment, as if the light were a friend he wanted to greet coming into the room, and then something lifted up off him. Not a solid thing, not a weight, but something washed out of him, a worry, a pain, a fear, and when he turned back to the window the girl was gone. There was just the night and the rain.

'I'm home,' called Mrs Shuffleup as she pushed open the front door. 'Amanda? Marigold? The storm was too bad. Ruth couldn't leave her little Simon on his own, stupid dog, and Mr Stott was afraid Bishops Road was going to flood again, so the meeting's postponed, which is silly because—'

'Mum!' Amanda said, running into the hall. 'There was this power cut and the lights went out and there was this girl in your study and she was dead creepy and—'

'Slow down, love,' her mum said, hanging her coat up on the hatstand by the radiator. 'What's all this?'

Goldie came out into the hall.

'Hi, Mrs Shuffleup. We were playing hide and seek and there was a power cut, that's all. Amanda was in the study there, and she thought she saw something in the lightning. She didn't half scare me with her screaming—'

'I did *not* scream,' Amanda interrupted, defending her honour angrily. 'I'm no scaredy-cat.'

'I'm sure you didn't, love,' her mum said, sitting down on the stairs and pulling Amanda close for a cuddle.

Amanda struggled away.

'There was this girl, right. The same one I saw this afternoon, and she—'

'Oh, you do let your imagination run away sometimes, don't you?'

'No,' Amanda protested. 'I didn't *imagine* her, she was—'

'There was no one there,' Goldie said, cutting in. 'We looked

54

everywhere and there was nowhere to hide in there…except…
except under the desk.'

Amanda clenched her mouth anxiously. She had a sudden
sinking feeling in her stomach.

'And *that* was where Amanda was hiding! Ha! Found you!'

'It doesn't count,' Amanda snapped. 'You *didn't* find me. You
didn't. Tell her, Mum.'

'I helped you out from where you'd got tangled up with the
chair. I pulled you out of your hiding place. I *definitely* found you.
I win.'

'It's not fair,' Amanda said. 'I'm going to go find Rudger.'

Rudger was sat on the messed-up bed. He'd shut the window,
but his T-shirt was still untucked and his hair looked unusually
spiky. When he saw Amanda he said, 'You'll never believe what
happened. All the lights went out and there was this girl. The one
you saw with that man. The *imaginary* one.'

'Yeah, I know *that*,' Amanda said, dismissively, as if it were old
news. 'I saw her downstairs.'

'She attacked me,' Rudger said. 'Tried to drag me out the window—'

Amanda looked at him, but wasn't really listening. The
babysitter had cheated. The unfairness of it filled her head.

'Do you know what happened?' she said, ignoring Rudger's
story. 'That Goldie reckons she found me, even though I'd already
come out of hiding. Can you believe that?'

Rudger stood there with his mouth open for a moment before saying, 'Did you hear what I said? The girl, the scary-looking one with the hair and the hissing, she *attacked* me. It was horrible. Her hands were all—'

'Oh, stop exaggerating. You always make such a fuss about everything. I saw her downstairs and she wasn't *that* scary.'

'You didn't have her touch you, I'll bet.' Rudger shivered at the memory. 'Her hands. Ugh. They were all cold and clammy. All wrong. It was just horrible.'

'Rudger,' Amanda said, sounding suddenly shocked, 'you've knocked my moneybox over.'

Rudger hadn't even noticed it. Her moneybox, shaped like a red pillar box with a slot in the top, had been a birthday present from Granny and Grandad Shuffleup. It lay on the floor, broken, and coins had spilled out.

'Sorry,' he stuttered. 'I guess *she* must've knocked it over when she climbed onto the windowsill.'

'Whatever,' Amanda said, waving his explanation away and brushing past him. She knelt down at the edge of the bed and began picking up the money.

Rudger stared, his heart beating oddly, hollowly in his chest.

'I could've been dragged out the window,' he said slowly, watching her clutch her coins, 'kidnapped by some imaginary ghost-girl, and you're…you're not even listening to me.'

She was driving him mad. Driving him crazy. She was supposed to be his friend, to be his best friend, and she wouldn't even listen to him. He'd just had the most terrifying experience of his short life (two months, three weeks and a day) and what did she care about? Some spilled coins and a stupid game of hide and seek. That wasn't how a friend was supposed to behave, was it? She should have said how sorry she was and asked what she could do to make him feel better. But instead she picked up the last few coins and put them in a pile on her bedside cabinet, before turning and flashing him the sort of smile a hungry spider gives a tired fly.

What now? he thought.

'There you are,' Amanda said pointing at him. 'That's the most rubbish hiding place I've ever seen. Amanda wins!'

She pumped the air with her fist, like a winner.

'Hang on,' Rudger said, 'that's not fair. I didn't think we were still playing.'

'I never said we *weren't*,' Amanda explained, 'and so I win.'

'I've had enough of this,' he said. 'I'm going to my wardrobe.'

He walked across the bedroom, stepped inside his wardrobe and shut the door behind him. *That'll teach her a lesson*, he thought.

FOUR

'Can we go swimming today, Mum?' Amanda asked the next morning.

She waved her spoon at the window. It had stopped raining out there, but the morning light was grey like dishwater, the rain pooled in huge puddles and drops were dripping from the blocked gutters. 'We can't go play in the garden, and me and Rudger ain't been swimming for ages.'

Rudger looked at her. It seemed she hadn't noticed that he wasn't talking to her.

'I suppose so,' her mum said. 'I've got to go into town anyway, so maybe we could…'

'Brilliant!'

Gobbling the last spoonful of her cornflakes noisily, Amanda jumped down from the table and ran upstairs.

Her mum picked her bowl up, then stacked Rudger's on top of it. She tipped his uneaten cornflakes into the bin.

She rubbed her eyes tiredly, put the bowls in the sink, turned on the hot tap and squirted a dribble of washing-up liquid into the water.

Rudger went out to wait in the hall.

He'd teach Amanda a lesson. He'd wait until she noticed he was upset and apologised to him, and *then* he'd forgive her and everything could be as it was before.

It was a plan and he was going to stick to it.

She ran downstairs with sparkling eyes and her rucksack in her hands.

'I've got my costume and goggles and some towels and I got a pair of shorts for you. Let's see if Mum's ready yet.'

By the time Rudger didn't reply, Amanda had already run into the kitchen.

The problem with Amanda, Rudger realised, was that she didn't *notice* things.

She hadn't noticed his fear last night and she didn't notice his silence this morning. She was off in her own world, nattering away as if Rudger was hanging on her every word, which of course he was, waiting for her apology. But as hard as he listened, none of the hundreds of words she threw into the air were the 'sorry' he longed for.

And although a silence is as silent as it can get, Rudger's silence still managed to grow even more so with each passing moment. Just because she'd imagined him didn't mean she could ignore his feelings.

He folded his arms and looked out of the car window.

On the pavement across from the house, under the opposite neighbour's tree, he thought for a moment he saw two figures just standing there, but as Amanda's mum reversed out of the drive, the car turned in such a way that he could no longer see them. By the time he'd swivelled to look out of the rear window, they'd gone.

Should he tell Amanda? But what could he say? She'd just take the mickey. If she hadn't noticed them, then maybe they hadn't been there. She was usually so good at noticing things, except, of course, he corrected himself, when she wasn't. He kept quiet.

Upon reflection, he thought, it *must* have been a trick of the light, just a memory from the night before echoing in his mind. He hadn't slept very well, tossing and turning in his wardrobe, and now he gave a big yawn.

'I've always preferred the backstroke,' Amanda was saying, not noticing anything much but the sound of her own voice,

'because you don't get the water in your eyes so much that way. I've always reckoned that they should paint pictures on the ceiling, or maybe a comic strip or something, so you can read it as you swim. D'you agree?'

She kept on talking to him, even though his arms were crossed and his eyes were glued to the window.

'I'm probably the *fourth* best swimmer in my class. Vincent's better than me 'cos he's got longer legs, and Taylor's got a face like a fish, so she's better than almost anyone. And I've never seen Absalom swim, so I don't know if he's better or not. Maybe I'm *third* best. What do you think, Rudger?'

There was a gap while she waited for Rudger's answer, which he didn't give, and then she went on again.

'What I like best of all's the smell. It's sort of weird, isn't it? And the sound of it. It's like a church full of water, or a bus station perhaps. It *echoes*. And the smell is odd but nice. Some people don't like it. Julia says it stings her eyes, but that's the sort of thing she would say, isn't it, because she's allergic to peanuts.'

Rudger felt *so* annoyed with her. His anger was stuck inside him and he felt his ears might pop off at any moment and let out great gushes of steam. And all she could do was blather on.

'Aren't you even going to say sorry?' he blurted out when she finally paused for breath.

Amanda turned to look at him with her mouth open.

'What are you talking about?' she asked in a quieter voice so her mum couldn't hear. 'What do you mean, say sorry?'

This time Rudger's jaw dropped. After all this, after a whole morning of the silent treatment, of his cold shoulder, she genuinely didn't know *why* he was upset. She hadn't even noticed.

'*What*?' she whispered.

'Last night,' he said.

'Oh, that!' Amanda breezily waved her hand in the air. 'I've forgiven you for that *ages* ago.'

Rudger stamped his feet in frustration.

'No, no, no,' he said, gritting his teeth. 'That's not fair. *You* can't forgive *me*. That's not how it works.'

'How would you know how it works?' Amanda said shortly, having grown tired of the conversation. 'You're *my* 'maginary friend, Rudger, not the other way round. I've been alive for *ages* more than you. You're only two months and three weeks and two days old. You know *nothing*. Without me thinking of stuff all the time you'd probably just…I don't know, fade away or something.'

'You alright back there, darling?' Amanda's mum called over her shoulder.

'Yes, Mum,' Amanda said cheerily.

'That's not true. I can't fade,' Rudger said, thinking it probably was.

'Is too,' Amanda hissed.

'Hmmph.'

Amanda's mum stopped the car. They'd arrived at the swimming pool.

'Don't forget your bag, darling.'

Amanda unbuckled her seatbelt, lifted her rucksack from between her feet and opened the car door. She climbed out.

Rudger slid over the seat and got out of the same door and then they were stood on the tarmac between two parked cars.

'Wait here, Amanda, guard the car for a sec. I'll just pop across and get a ticket.'

Mrs Shuffleup shouldered her handbag and headed off to the ticket machine to pay for their parking.

Rudger stepped out from between the cars. Although their argument, the argument he was entirely on the right side of, had been interrupted, now they were on their own he wasn't going to let it go.

'If that's what you think,' he said, meaning that he'd fade without Amanda around to imagine him, 'then maybe we should put it to the test. Maybe I'll go off for a bit and show you I don't need you.' He walked across the roadway and stood between the two parked cars opposite. He held his hands up so they could both see them. 'Look, I'm not fading yet.'

'Don't be silly, Rudger,' Amanda said, holding out her hand to him. 'Come back here.'

'Not until you say sorry.'

Amanda sighed. Took a deep breath. She didn't want to lose Rudger. Vincent and Julia were good friends, but only Rudger was her *best* friend. He was the one she could share the wild adventures with. Only an imaginary friend could do that. The others tried, but they could only *pretend*. Rudger was the real deal.

'I'm sorry,' she said. 'Look, I'm sorry I've upset you.'

Then, in a quick surprising dart, with just the sort of sudden leap that had saved her from tigers and aliens all summer, she ran out from between the cars intent on giving Rudger a friendly punch on the arm (she was not the sort of girl who hugged).

She reached him a split second before an old blue car screeched, smoked and shuddered to a halt exactly where she'd just run. If she'd been slower or had started running a moment later, she'd be flat like toast right now, knocked down by the car, run over while running over to Rudger.

Her heart was beating faster than she could remember. It hammered in her chest. She hadn't run far, just a matter of metres, but she was strangely, unexpectedly out of breath.

She felt cold, as if the sun had suddenly gone behind a cloud. Looking up, she saw the sun had gone behind a cloud.

'Oh, Amanda,' Rudger said putting his arm round her, 'that car …that car…it almost hit you.'

'Little girl,' said the driver climbing out, his worried voice wavering. 'I didn't see you run out. I got such a fright, a dreadful fright. Are you intact? Are you unhurt? Is your dear mother nearby in the vicinity?'

Rudger and Amanda looked up together and saw a large tall bald man leaning with one hand on his open car door. His red moustache fluttered with each word and his Hawaiian shirt looked out of place on such a damp, grey morning.

'It's him, isn't it?' Rudger said.

Amanda caught her breath and said, 'Yes.' Then to the man she said loudly, 'She'll be back in a second, me mum. She's getting a ticket. And thank you very much for not running me over, but I'm all right now.'

The man nodded. 'Good,' he said. 'I'm glad that you came to no harm. I have no wish to hurt you. In fact, as it happens, I have no interest in you at all. But I see your friend.' He looked at Rudger. (Rudger had never been seen by a grownup before. He felt slightly sick.) 'And I notice…' The man, Amanda remembered him saying his name was Mr Bunting, lifted himself on tiptoe and looked back across the tops of the parked cars. '…that there is rather a queue at the car park pay and display ticketing machine. I suspect your mother will be a little while yet.'

Rudger didn't know what made him turn round. It wasn't a crunch of gravel, because no gravel crunched; it wasn't a scent carried on the breeze, because she wore no perfume; it wasn't even a feeling that suddenly weighed his heart down, because…well, maybe it *was*

something like that. Whatever the cause, Rudger turned to look behind him, down the passage between the parked cars, and he saw her.

She was stood at the end of the car-walled alleyway, still and silent. She looked as if she was blocking their only means of escape, but she wasn't.

'Amanda, run!' Rudger shouted, pushing her out past the big man. 'Get to your mum!'

Amanda saw the sense and, without looking back, ran past Mr Bunting's blue car. She skidded her hand across its damp bonnet and sprinted up the ginnel between her mum's car and the next, heading over towards the ticket machine. She was sure Mr Bunting and the girl wouldn't follow if they knew they were running to her mum. They'd be safe with her. Wouldn't they?

But then she glanced behind and saw she was on her own. Rudger wasn't there. And she paused for a moment, and saw that *no one* was there. No one had followed her. Not just Rudger, but no one else either.

Rudger pushed Amanda, sending her running off. He'd meant to set off after her and get away from the odd couple, but a cold hand snapped round his wrist before he could take a step.

The girl had moved faster than seemed possible, the whole length of two cars in the blink of an eye, and her grip on him was tight. He kicked out, but that didn't help, and then she had his other wrist.

Although he struggled, her hold on him was cold and draining. It was as if she'd injected him with some sort of soothing but nightmarish drug, as if he were a fish she'd landed, whisked out of his element and left to flounder hopelessly on dry earth. He fell numb, limp and dirty.

He was kneeling in a puddle. His knees were cold, but hardly colder than his insides. He tried to push the girl off him, to kick out, but his attempts, while being tough and manly in his mind, landed on her like the blows of a jellyfish fighting off a shark.

And then a shadow fell across his face.

The man, Mr Bunting, was kneeling down, like a man might kneel to do up his shoelace, and his moustache was ruffling. It's funny, Rudger thought, when you're in a sticky situation, facing who knows what sort of fate, the things you notice. Mr Bunting's moustache was ruffling, but he wasn't speaking.

Instead, he opened his mouth up, wider than any normal person would open their mouth, unhinged it almost, snake-like, and a hot breath wafted into Rudger's face. It smelt like a desert might smell, dry and reddish and rotten with spice. It cut through the damp air, the overcast grey sky, the puddled tarmac. It filled Rudger's world.

With his mouth open so widely, so weirdly, Rudger saw that Mr Bunting's teeth weren't like those of a normal person. They were blunt and square, identical to one another, and circled round and round. They ran back and back into his head in neat rows. In fact, Rudger thought, it looked like a white-tiled tunnel running

off into the far distance, with a pinprick of pitch darkness at the end of it. It went so far it should have come out of the back of Mr Bunting's head, but obviously it didn't, that would be mad. It went, instead, which Rudger realised was no less mad, *somewhere else*.

And then the dry spicy wind that had been blowing gently into his face vanished. Mr Bunting began to suck, and at the same time the girl let Rudger go and scuttled away. He lay there on the tarmac, his back against the cold hubcap of a car wheel, and felt something of himself being dragged up, being pulled along with the wind.

He felt as if the world had tipped on its edge and instead of being a tunnel leading off into some unknown distance, Mr Bunting's mouth had become a pit, a hole, a shaft or well that he was on the very edge of falling into.

And then he heard a voice he knew and loved calling his name.

Amanda saw Mr Bunting leaning over Rudger. The weird silent girl was huddled to one side, staring blankly at them, but slowly rubbing her hands together.

Amanda ran at them and she kicked the large man's ankle as hard as she could. Twice.

He huffed and puffed as he heaved himself upright. He put a hand out to lean on the bumper of the car beside him. The car creaked and wobbled under his weight. Mr Bunting slowly turned to face her, a smirk underneath his bushy moustache.

'You came back, little Amanda,' Mr Bunting said slowly, horribly. 'How very sweet you are. How kindly.'

Rudger scrambled up on to his feet, and, dodging round the big man's legs, grabbed hold of Amanda's arm, and they ran.

They ran together.

They ran, away from Mr Bunting and the girl, ducking down between cars, heading back the way Amanda had come, over to where the ticket machine was.

Amanda didn't dare look round. Through a break in the cars to her left she saw something dark flit past, something fast, something keeping up with them a row over. It was the girl, she just knew it, but this time Rudger was in front of her, she knew he was safe and she kept running. They had to get to her mum.

Thunder grumbled above them and the first spots of rain hit their faces as they ran. And then she and Rudger burst out from between the last pair of cars and from their right, the way they weren't looking, a moving car came out of nowhere.

It wasn't going fast, just pootling round the car park, but sometimes slow is fast enough.

Rudger bounced off the bonnet and rolled with a thump to the ground. He hit his elbow and scuffed his knee, but it didn't hurt, not much. He clambered to his feet, knocking gravel off his jeans with his hands.

'Amanda,' he said, looking round. 'Amanda?'

She was on the ground. She'd been knocked over too. Her head rested on the tarmac in a small dark puddle. Her eyes were shut.

Her left arm was thrown out above her head at an unusual angle. She looked peaceful, but weird. Then he realised he couldn't see her breathing.

Was she breathing? He couldn't tell.

Before he could run to her there were people everywhere.

The driver of the car had opened her door, was staggering, saying, 'She just ran out in front of me… I couldn't stop… She just ran out.' Her face was grey. There were tears on her cheeks.

Someone was phoning an ambulance. Someone was listening to Amanda's chest, was holding the wrist of the arm that wasn't bent oddly. Someone was pointing back the way they'd come, where they'd run from, saying something.

The rain fell, harder now.

And then Amanda's mum was there, crying, lifting Amanda up. Someone tried to stop her, saying she shouldn't be moved, but her mum knelt on the tarmac and held her and stroked her hair.

And then the crowd of people blocked them from Rudger's sight and because they couldn't see him, he got nudged out of the way, further back.

And then the ambulance came and Amanda went away.

FIVE

There was a hole in the middle of Rudger. A hole where his heart had been, or where he'd imagined it to be, or where Amanda had imagined it to be. He was hollow now, echoing like an empty can.

When he looked around he found he was still in the car park. The ambulance had gone ages before. Mr Bunting and the girl had vanished, scared off by the crowd perhaps. And now most of the cars were gone too. Amanda's mum's car was still there. She'd gone off in the ambulance. Would she come back for it? What did people do when such terrible things happened?

Rudger didn't know.

There was so much Rudger didn't know. He didn't know the way home. He didn't know if he still had a home. He didn't know if he would be welcome in Amanda's house without Amanda.

What good would it do him to be there if Amanda wasn't there to see him?

What would Amanda's mum do in an empty house? To be all alone is a dreadful thing. He thought of the photographs of Amanda and her mum on the hallway wall, and of the one of her mum and her dad before he'd died, right back before Amanda was born. He thought of the pictures of her grandparents and her aunts and uncles. All photos of other people. There were none of him. None of Rudger.

Without Amanda there to see him, it wouldn't be his house any more, would it?

He lifted his hands up. They weren't see-through, not exactly. He hadn't simply faded away like Amanda said he would, but they were definitely greyer, definitely fainter than they'd been before. There was something smoky about them. When he moved them quickly they left a wisp of a trail behind them.

The day had moved on without him noticing. The clouds had disappeared and the sun was now sinking behind the swimming pool. Shadows were creeping across the tarmac. As long as he stood in the car park the things that had happened there played in his head like a film. He had to get away. If he was to think straight, if he was to come up with a plan, if he was to work out what to do next, he needed to put the car park behind him.

And so, because he had to do *something*, and because he didn't know what, Rudger ran.

He jogged past the last few cars and ran between the last swimmers leaving the pool. (They didn't see him, but felt the rush of wind curl between them as he ran by, and wondered at the faint grey gunpowder smell in the air.)

He ran down the path at the side of the big building. His lungs were fiery and his legs ached, but he kept running. The spiral tube of the water slide passed by overhead, and neat flowerbeds passed by on the other side. Gravel crunched under his feet. He dodged a pothole, jumped a puddle and suddenly he was running on grass.

Behind the swimming pool, at the end of the path he'd run along, was the town park.

It was green and wide and the sight of such a fresh open space lifted him for a second. It was just the sort of place Amanda could have, and would have, dreamt into becoming a whole new huge world. He stopped running and leant on his knees. No matter how hard he looked at the park, no matter what he wished it to become, it stayed a park. He didn't have the spark in his head that she'd had in hers. He didn't have the imagination needed to imagine new worlds.

In fact, he thought, feeling a strange faint tingling, he didn't even have the imagination to imagine himself.

He held his hands up and saw the outlines of trees through them. He saw the greens of trees through them too, faint, greyish greens, but greens nonetheless. He was fading away. Without

75

Amanda to think of him, to remember him, to dream him, to make him real, he was slipping away.

Rudger was being forgotten. He was disappearing. Evaporating.

He walked into the shade of a tree and touched its thick patchwork bark with his fingertip. It looked rough, gnarled, hard, but it was like marshmallow. His faint fading finger hardly felt it at all.

He slumped on the grass with his back to the tree trunk. It was comfortable. It was like resting on a pillow.

He was fading all over now.

He felt sleepy and sleepier.

He shut his eyes.

What would it be like to fade away? To vanish entirely?

Time would tell, he thought, soon enough, time would tell.

'I can see you,' said a voice.

Rudger looked up.

Who'd said that?

At first he didn't see the black shape. It had grown dark under the tree. Night was falling, and the cat was simply a darker cat-shaped shape in the darkness.

A *cat*?

Had a cat just spoken to him?

He said nothing, unsure of what one should say to a cat.

'Little boy,' the cat said. 'I *can* see you.'

At Rudger's back the tree was suddenly uncomfortable. The cushioniness of it had snapped back into the usual expected rough barkiness. He lifted his hands. It was hard to tell in the half-light of the evening, but they looked, and they certainly felt, like real fingers again. They'd lost their wispiness, their haze.

'You can see me?' he said, feeling a little foolish.

'Oh, I see you,' the cat said.

'But no one ever sees me.'

'Someone must do. Someone must have. I know your sort. I know what you are.'

'Who are you?' Rudger asked. '*What* are you?'

'Me? I'm Zinzan.'

'Zinzan,' Rudger repeated, trying out the unfamiliar name.

'Yes,' the cat said. 'And do you have a name? I could just call you "boy", but there are so many boys in the world it would become confusing.'

'I'm called Rudger,' Rudger said.

'Hmm.'

Rudger wished he could see the cat's expression. It was too dark to make anything out. Its voice sounded haughty, a touch bored, as if it wanted to be somewhere else, as if it had something better to be doing. He didn't know if the cat *was* bored, if it *did* have somewhere better to be, or whether that was just how cats sounded. He'd never heard a cat talk before. As far as he knew no one had.

He wondered if someone was playing a trick on him, but then who *could* play a trick on him? You'd have to see him first, and the only person who'd ever seen him had been Amanda. (And, he remembered with a lurch, Mr Bunting.)

As he thought of Amanda he felt himself begin to fade again.

'Oh no you don't,' Zinzan said. 'I believe in you, Rudger. And I'm not going to have you Fade on me.' Rudger noticed the way the cat said the word, with a capital 'F' as if it were a medical condition. 'It's tricky, isn't it, these first few days? Being forgotten? But it happens to you all, sooner or later. Come with me. Come on.'

'I've not been forgotten,' Rudger answered, half-angry. 'Not *forgotten*.' He softened his voice. It wasn't the cat's fault and besides his heart was weighing the words down. 'There was an accident. Amanda got knocked down, she was…' He paused before he reached the word he meant to say, and then said a different one. '…hurt.'

The cat said nothing.

'I think…' Rudger went on haltingly, finding the words hard to say, but wanting to say them, needing to say them all the same. 'I think she's…dead. They took her away. And I was left on my own.'

'No,' said Zinzan casually. 'I've seen what happens when someone dies, seen what happens to someone like you. They die; you vanish, like shutting a door. Gone in a second. No, you…you're just *Fading*, boy, and Fading means you're being forgotten, that's all.'

Rudger's heart began to beat again. 'She's alive?'

'Evidently so, or I wouldn't be speaking to you.'

'Then I've got to find her. I've got to go to her.'

'And how will you do that, little Will-o'-the-wisp? Five minutes on your own and you'll blow away on the breeze. I've no time to look for your girl, but I won't leave you to Fade. I'm not heartless. I'll take you somewhere safe, somewhere useful.'

And with those words the cat turned and trotted off through the long grass, away from the tree and didn't once look behind to see if Rudger was following.

What choice did Rudger have?

No choice.

He scrambled to his feet and followed.

Rudger followed the cat through the park, out of the gate and down the street.

'Hey, slow down,' he called.

The cat didn't slow.

It padded along the street, weaving unnoticed through the legs of passers-by, before sidling into an alleyway opposite a garishly lit kebab shop. Purple lights reflected in puddles at the alley's mouth.

Rudger hurried after the cat, afraid that it would be gone when he got there, that he'd be stranded in an alley with no clue as to what to do next.

But there it was, sat on top of a dustbin, rubbing its ears with its wrists.

A flickering streetlight cast a pale glow over the bin and over the cat. This was the first good look Rudger had got at his…at his what? His new friend? His saviour? His new problem? It was hard to say.

From the ring of Zinzan's voice Rudger had assumed he was dealing with a cat of refinement, a gentleman, an aristocrat. If he had known anything of cat breeds, which he didn't, he would've pictured a Siamese or a Burmese. But what sat on the bin before him looked more like a cat put together from the leftover parts of several other cats who'd been in a war, all on the losing side.

Its fur was matted in places and missing in others. Its tail bent at a right angle halfway down. Its right eye was red and the left was blue. Parts of it were brown and parts were white and some parts Rudger couldn't begin to guess the colour of without first offering the cat a bath. And Zinzan didn't look the sort of cat you could bathe without a great deal of effort, soap and courage.

Zinzan looked like nothing less than a boxer, a bruiser, a brute. A dangerous person to know.

And he was, Rudger also realised, in fact hadn't stopped realising as he took this all in, the *only* person Rudger knew. Until he got back to Amanda, that was.

'What happens now?'

'I take you somewhere you'll be safe,' the cat replied, its tone suggesting that this was obvious.

'Where?'

'Oh, hereabouts,' the cat said slowly, gazing round the alley as if looking for something. 'It's just a case of finding the right door at the right time.'

'What does *that* mean?'

The cat yawned. Its teeth glinted yellowly (the ones that weren't missing).

'So many questions,' it said, before yawning again. 'I'm merely a helper, Rudger. A Good Samaritan. If I had the answers, well, do you think I'd look like this?'

'I don't know,' Rudger said. 'That's why I asked. Amanda always asks questions.'

'And does she always get answers?'

Rudger thought.

'No, not always.'

'And when she doesn't get answers?'

'She makes it up, usually.'

Zinzan laughed. It was a strange laugh, somewhere between a purr and a cough, but it wasn't cruel.

'That's probably why she thought of you,' the cat said. 'As the answer to a question she got no other answer to.'

It licked its shoulder, twitched its whiskers and jumped down from the bin.

'Come,' it said. 'I smell a door opening. Follow me.'

And with that it ran further into the alley, off into the dark.

One alley led to another alley and that alley led to a third and the third led on to a fourth.

It was hard to see Zinzan up ahead, but the cat said, 'Come on,' and, 'This way,' and, 'I see you,' just often enough for Rudger to not lose track of it.

He had the most peculiar feeling that they'd run down *too many* alleyways. An alley had to lead somewhere, lead you back out to a street, surely? With Zinzan, however, alley led to alley led to alley. But it was dark and it was late and Rudger was tired and today had been dreadful, so he just followed the cat and pushed any doubts he had to the back of his head.

One thing he knew though, for sure: if he had been lost before, he was impossibly lost now.

'Here we are,' Zinzan said, stopping suddenly.

'Where?' asked Rudger. It looked exactly like the alley they'd started in. It even opened out on to the same road they'd come in from. Rudger could see the neon sign of the kebab shop opposite.

'At the door to your new life,' the cat replied, licking a paw and rubbing it across its nose.

'What door?' Rudger asked, looking round. 'I don't see it.'

'Ah,' Zinzan said, between licks of its tail. 'But I see it.'

As the cat spoke a light flickered into life on the wall beside them. It lit a plain wooden door. The door stood slightly ajar but Rudger could see nothing of what was on the other side.

'You should go in,' Zinzan said. 'I can't look at you forever. I have things to be doing. Important things. I smell mouse. I've got work to do. Go on. Get.'

Hesitantly Rudger pushed the door.

Rudger was in a passage, like you'd find in an old house, lined with wallpaper patterned with tiny blue flowers. The floorboards creaked and groaned under his feet. Although there was a cool draught from the open door behind him, the corridor was warm and musty. He thought it smelt of old things, furry things, smelt like a damp dog snoring in front of a fire.

At the other end of the corridor was a second door. It too was ajar and he could hear a faint tinkle of music coming from it. Rudger walked forwards. It was either that or go back to the alley, and the cat had made it clear it wasn't going to hang around waiting.

He went on.

He could definitely hear music, though it was still faint, and there were other noises too. He could hear voices, distant voices. He couldn't make out any words, but there were people somewhere round here.

He sat down on the floor with his back to the wall and listened.

Rudger was afraid.

Amanda had always seen him, but none of her friends did. Her mum didn't see him. The neighbours who lived either side of Amanda's house had never seen him. He'd had to climb over their fences on more than one occasion to get a lost ball or Frisbee or fizzing stick of dynamite, and they'd never said a word to him. How would he feel if he went through that door and found a whole roomful of people to ignore him? Or worse, a room of Mr Buntings who *could* see him?

Zinzan had said he'd be safe here, but Zinzan was a cat. What do cats know?

But, Rudger argued, the cat *had* seen him. The cat had stopped him from Fading. The cat had told him about Amanda, about her still being alive. Maybe he *should* trust the cat.

He stood up. He could do this. What would Amanda have done if she'd been in his shoes? Probably complained that her shoes were too big, but after that she'd've gone through the door and faced whatever was on the other side. Rudger took a leaf from her book, a lesson from everything they'd shared together, and he pushed the door.

It shut with a click.

He pushed again and it didn't move.

So he turned the handle and *pulled* it and the door opened to reveal almost the last thing he'd thought to find.

SIX

Rudger was in a library.

Amanda had told him about them, but he'd never seen one before. She'd said, 'It's the best sort of indoors there is for a rainy day. Every book is an adventure,' and she loved adventures.

The music he'd heard was louder now. It crackled and popped as if it were being played on an old gramophone, but it was lively, happy, cheering.

He couldn't see where it was coming from because there were bookcases in the way. They were all over the place. The library was a maze, he thought, a labyrinth built of books.

He looked around. Ten metres away, up the aisle to his right, a yawning woman was pushing a little trolley piled high with books.

As he watched she stopped, pulled a pair of hardbacks off the trolley, looked at them, then at the shelf, and then slid them carefully into their right places.

'Hello?' Rudger said.

She ignored him, pulled the trolley back a few steps and shelved some more books. She didn't hurry, even though it was late and she should probably have been getting home, but carefully put them exactly where they belonged.

'What are you talking to her for?' a little voice said from somewhere above him. 'She's real. She can't see you.'

Rudger looked up.

Peering over the bookcase was the huge-toothed head of a dinosaur, possibly a tyrannosaur of some sort. Rudger was no expert, but he could tell at the very least that it wasn't a herbivore: its teeth were huge, long, yellow and pointed. It snurfed through its great dark nostrils, licked a thick glistening tongue over its lipless lips and blinked its tiny eyes before speaking again.

'Have you just arrived?' it asked. Its voice was quiet, high like a child's, not a monster's, although its teeth clattered unnervingly each time it spoke.

Rudger wasn't sure what to say.

It wasn't that he was scared. Not really. But he was surprised.

Three things made the encounter less frightening than it might otherwise have been. Firstly, the dinosaur had to duck awkwardly to fit in under the library's ceiling, which looked funny. Secondly, its tiny arms were resting on the top of the bookcase it was looking over, and a tyrannosaur's tiny arms *always* look funny. And thirdly, it was pink.

'Um,' Rudger said. 'Yes, I'm new here.'

'I knew it. I knew it,' the dinosaur said, trying to clap its small hands together and failing. 'Come round here, you need to meet everyone.'

It was like walking into a cartoon after spending a day in a subtitled black and white French film, Rudger thought. The dinosaur, with its startling colour, wasn't the only oddity there.

In the middle of the library, where the bookcases gave way to tables and chairs, 'people' were gathered. Rudger used the word 'people' loosely as he looked at them, and left the word 'real' out of his thoughts entirely.

He was in a room full of *imaginary* people. There were some who looked like ordinary kids, like he did, and there were others who didn't. There was a person-sized teddy bear and there was a clown and there was a man who looked like a Victorian schoolmaster, lean and pale and severe. There was a drifting patch of colour the exact shade of a summer's sky and there was a tiny gnomish fellow hiding behind another tiny gnomish fellow who was trying to hide behind the first one and there was a ragdoll slumped in a chair (which Rudger learnt later was just a ragdoll some kid had lost in the library earlier that day).

Even the gramophone from which the music drifted was an imaginary person. It had short arms and legs sticking out of it and a pair of eyes that span round on the record, blinking each time they went under the stylus. When it saw Rudger the music crackled to a halt. It coughed politely, lifted its stylus arm up and blinked several times.

For a moment Rudger just stared at them all. He'd only ever seen one imaginary person before, and she'd tried to drag him out of the window and feed him to Mr Bunting. Now he was faced by a throng of them he felt overwhelmed.

'You look lost,' said a teenage girl.

She was wearing dungarees. Rudger had never seen dungarees before. He was very good and didn't giggle.

'He's just come in,' said the dinosaur, turning round with difficulty under the low ceiling. 'He came in from the Corridor.'

'Come over here,' said the girl, taking his elbow and walking him away from all the others. 'Have a seat. You're probably confused. Your first time here?'

'Yes,' said Rudger, sitting on a sofa next to a rack of children's picture books. 'Where am I? Who are all those…um…people?'

'We call it the Agency,' she said sitting down next to him. 'And who are *they*?' She spread her hands to indicate the whole lot of them. 'I guess you could say they're your family. Welcome home!'

The girl was called Emily.

'Do you want a cup of tea, or a hot chocolate, or something like that?' she asked.

The teddy bear pushed a trolley brimming with drinks and cakes over towards them. One of the wheels squeaked.

'Um, hot chocolate, please,' Rudger said.

'Here you go,' said the bear, handing him a steaming mug. 'Cake?'

Rudger was surprised how hungry he was. He didn't normally eat much. Amanda kindly finished off whatever he left and she usually encouraged him to leave the lot. It had become a habit.

'Can I have one of those?' he asked, pointing at a little cupcake.

The bear handed it to him, with a napkin. He picked a few strands of fur off the icing and took a bite.

'Good, now you've got yourself a cake,' Emily said, 'I'd best give you The Talk.'

'The Talk?' Rudger asked, spitting crumbs.

The teddy bear trundled the squeaking trolley away as Emily wiped crumbs off the bib of her dungarees.

'Yeah, The Talk. It's what everyone gets when they come through that door for the first time. You're frightened, you're scared, you've been forgotten, you've been Fading and then, just before you blow away on the wind, you find a magic door and next thing you know you're being stared at by Snowflake.'

'Snowflake?'

Emily pointed at the pink dinosaur, who was playing cards with some other imaginary friends. It was having difficulty seeing what cards it had in its hand. The tip of its tail was tapping the bookcase behind it in annoyance.

'Of course, not everyone gets stared at by Snowflake. Depends who's around at the time. We do try to be friendly.'

'What *is* this place?'

'This, Rudge,' she said, shortening his name annoyingly, 'is a place for people like us to hang out between jobs.'

'Jobs?'

Emily took a deep breath before launching into the explanation. 'Here's how it is,' she said. 'Some kids have big imaginations and they dream us up. They make us and we're best chums and that's all good and proper, and then they get older and they lose interest and we get forgotten. That's when we start to Fade. Normally that's the end, your job's done, you turn to smoke and blow away on the wind. But if *we* find you before that happens, or if one of our colleagues spots you, we can get you in here, where you'll be safe.'

'Why here?' Rudger asked.

Emily held her hands up and pointed to the shelves that surrounded them. 'You and me, Rudge, we're imagined. Look around, this place is like an oasis: it's *made* of imagination. Course, it's not *fresh*, but it's enough to keep you going for a few weeks.'

'Then what?'

'Then you've gotta go to work.'

'Work?'

Emily stood up.

Rudger stood up too. He put the cupcake wrapper in his pocket and held his half-empty hot chocolate mug warm in his hands.

'Come with me,' Emily said.

They walked through the maze of bookcases until they came to an open space at the front of the library. Here was the desk where the real people checked out their borrowed books during the day. In front of it was a sleeping dog. An imaginary sleeping dog, Rudger noticed. (Or a sleeping imaginary dog; he wasn't sure how the adjectives fitted.) There were a pair of glass doors that looked out onto the high street.

It was dark outside. The orange of a streetlight lit the pavement and a few people walked past under umbrellas. It was raining again.

The woman Rudger had seen pushing the trolley and shelving the books a little earlier unlocked the doors and went out, locking them behind her.

'That's the last of the reals gone home now,' Emily said. 'It's all ours until morning.'

On the wall at their side was a notice board, filled with the things library notice boards are usually filled with: adverts for book groups and babysitters; coffee mornings and art courses. As Rudger looked, though, something happened to them.

'That's it,' Emily said, 'you've just gotta relax and let your eyes see what they need to see.'

From behind all the flyers and posters, or maybe from in front of them, photographs began to appear. It was as if they had been hidden by a mist that was now being blown away by a wind he couldn't feel. Soon the board was covered with them.

'These are the children,' Emily said, pointing at the photos, 'who need Friends, or who want Friends, but who don't have enough imagination to dream one up. It's a rare kid who can do that, it takes a *really* sparky one.'

'Like Amanda?'

Emily nodded slowly.

'It's tough when they begin to forget, Rudge,' she said, 'but…'

'Oh, she's not forgotten me,' Rudger interrupted. 'It's just there was this accident. I'm going to find her and—'

'Rudge,' Emily said, before he could say any more. 'Slow down. Look, I'm sorry. I know it's hard, but I gotta tell it to you straight. You ain't gonna find her again. It don't work like that. I don't make the rules, but there *are* rules. This is just how it works. You get forgotten; then you pick a new one. There's no going back.'

Rudger didn't believe her, but he kept his mouth shut. He could tell he wasn't going to convince her, not there and then. Not tonight. (And besides, all the same, there was a voice flickering at the back of his mind, a little voice that said, 'But maybe she's right.')

There was a whimpering sound from behind them. Rudger turned and saw that the old sheepdog was dreaming. It gave a little snort and its feet twitched as if it were chasing a squirrel behind its eyelids.

'Don't mind him,' Emily said. Her voice softened as she talked about the dog, as if remembering good times long gone. 'He's waiting for his last job. Too old for his own good, he says. Says he's looking for something *really* special. Waits out here most of the time so as not to miss it when it turns up.'

'When what turns up?'

'Whatever kid it is he's looking for. I dunno. To be honest, he misses a lot of them by keeping watch while snoring, if you get my drift.'

Rudger looked at the old dog, chuckled nervously for a reason he couldn't quite put his finger on and then turned back to the notice board.

Emily carried on with The Talk.

'So you come down here in the morning,' she said, 'and you pick a kid you like the look of, and then you go up the Corridor and that's all there is to it.'

'That's all there is to it?'

'Yep, that's it.'

'How does it work?'

'Dunno,' Emily said with a shrug. 'It just does.' She paused before coughing and putting on an official-sounding voice, 'So, Rudge. You've had The Talk, as best as I can do it and now you're in the Imaginary business. Welcome aboard.' She raised an imaginary glass in an empty hand. 'Here's to loads of good jobs for years to come, eh? Let's go introduce you to the others.'

Later that evening Rudger was sitting beside a campfire in the middle of the library.

At first he'd been worried by this, fire and books not being best friends, but he saw that the fire was the sort of thing Amanda would have dreamt up. It was imagined. The library was in no danger of burning down, no books were being burnt, but still the imagined people sitting around it felt warm and looked kindly in the flickering firelight.

'It's the right thing for the evening,' Emily had said. 'It's what you're supposed to do. Toast a marshmallow and tell some ghost stories.'

The marshmallows were imagined too, but they tasted delicious, sticky and gooey. The library was a generous home, dreaming up all of this for them.

'That's one thing *we* can't do, Rudge,' Emily had explained. 'That's what the reals are for, dreaming stuff up. I bet your Amanda did it?'

'Yeah, every day.'

'Our job is to share it, to enjoy it. Guide it if you can, make suggestions, make requests, but you're always working with someone else's imagination. Remember that.'

He sipped another mug of hot chocolate and said nothing. He was thinking about Amanda. Emily's words from earlier were still rolling round his head. He was sure he'd be able to prove

her wrong. Maybe no other imaginary friend had made it back to their real friend before, their original friend, but that just meant he'd be the first.

He listened to the conversations going on around him. They were about people he didn't know who'd done things he didn't understand in places he'd never heard of with children he'd never met. After a while he decided he had to speak up.

He coughed.

'Excuse me,' he said.

The room fell silent, except for the rhythmic bouncing noise of a Friend who was the spitting image of a ping pong ball. (Rudger was more than glad Amanda had imagined him as an ordinary boy. It made things much easier.)

'I'm new here,' he said. 'As you know. Emily's been very helpful and has told me about how this place works. But…I don't…I don't think I'm meant to be here, not yet. There was an accident, you see.'

He began to tell the story, beginning the night before, when they'd been playing hide and seek with the babysitter.

'Did you say "Mr Bunting"?' Snowflake asked, from somewhere near the ceiling, when Rudger first mentioned the man.

'Yeah,' he said. 'That's what Amanda said his name was. She heard him tell her mum.'

'"Mr Bunting"?'

There was something funny about the way the dinosaur said the name. As if it were teasing him.

'What is it?' he said.

Emily put a hand on his shoulder and chuckled.

'Sorry, Rudge. We all know about Mr Bunting already. It's no good trying to make out you *met* him. You're not gonna fool us. Sorry to ruin your story.'

'No, but we *did* meet him. He tried to—'

The teddy bear, a girl called Cruncher-of-Bones, laughed.

'Oh yeah? Next you'll be saying you met Simple Simon.'

'Who's Simple Simon?'

'He's even scarier than Mr Bunting,' Emily said. 'He takes the place of your real friend in the night. Puts on their skin, looks at you through their eyes, and he tells you to do things. Weird things. Dangerous things. And because he says it in their voice, using their tongue to make the words, well…you have to do it.'

'Oh, be quiet, Emily,' said Snowflake. 'Simple Simon gives me the willies. I'll not be able to sleep tonight now you've put the thought in my head.' The dinosaur gnashed its great teeth together and shook as if a shiver were going up its spine. 'Brrr.'

'But it wasn't this Simple Simon bloke,' Rudger said, 'it was Mr Bunting. Tell me about him. What do you know?'

'Only what everyone knows, Rudge,' Emily said. 'He was born hundreds of years ago,' she went on, sounding as if she were reciting from an encyclopaedia, 'but he made a bargain with the devil. Blah, blah, blah.'

'I heard it was with pixies,' someone said.

'No, aliens,' said another.

'I thought it was with a bank manager,' said Cruncher-of-Bones.

'Well, I heard it was the devil, but it don't matter,' Emily went on. 'The point is, he just keeps on living. He don't die, even though he's hundreds of years old.'

'And what keeps him alive is...go on...' the ping pong ball urged between bounces.

'He eats imaginaries, Rudge. He eats people like us. And for each one he eats, he lives another year longer. That's what they say. But the stories don't say anything about him having a Friend.'

'Yes they do,' Snowflake said. 'What I heard was that he eats Friends to give himself enough imagination to keep believing in *his* Friend. Now he's a grownup, and has been for years and years, he should've forgotten her. But he doesn't want to, and the only way to keep believing is to eat...imagination.'

'I never heard that,' Emily said.

'How does he find Friends?' Rudger asked.

'Oh, he sniffs them out,' Cruncher-of-Bones answered. 'He can smell Fading, like cats do. Get a whiff of that up one nostril and he'll be on the trail like a bloodhound. And once he finds you it's cutlery out and eyes down for some speedy gobbling before you're all Faded away. Would you like another cake, Rudger?'

Rudger shook his head at the cake. He could smell Fading, eh? Well, that wasn't how he'd found Amanda's house and found him. Mr Bunting had been hunting for Friends then, not just waiting.

He'd been searching for them door-to-door. And from the moment Amanda had seen the girl on the doorstep Mr Bunting had known there was a girl living there who could see imaginary people, and that meant…

'Can he be killed?' he asked.

Emily looked at him. 'I don't remember any story where he got killed. Anyone?'

There was a general shaking of heads.

'Zinzan said,' Rudger said, 'that we just disappear if our children are killed. Is that true?'

'Yeah,' said Emily, chewing a marshmallow. 'And it happens the other way round too.'

'What do you mean?'

'If an imaginary dies, then the real friend dies too.'

'I've not heard that,' said the bouncing ping pong ball.

'It's true,' said Emily. 'There was this kid I heard of once. Him and his Friend, PikPik, fell off this cliff, yeah? They'd been mucking about and there was an accident. And they were falling, and PikPik hit the ground first. She smashed to pieces…vanished, poof! And then her real friend died too.'

There was a moment's silence before Snowflake said, 'But they'd fallen off a cliff. Of course the real friend died.'

'No,' said Emily, lowering her voice so everyone had to lean in to hear, 'you didn't listen proper. The imaginary died, *then* the real kid.'

'But they both fell from a great height,' Snowflake protested.

'Yeah, but the real kid was dead *before* it hit the ground.'

The silence dragged out a little longer before the dinosaur said, 'How do you know?'

Emily shrugged. 'That's just what I heard.'

It had grown late. The fire was dying down.

Some imaginaries were already heading off to bed.

Emily led Rudger between bookcases and down aisles until they reached one where there were hammocks slung from side to side.

'Here, let me give you a leg up,' she said, cupping her hands together and helping Rudger climb into the dangling bed.

He'd spent all his life sleeping in the bottom of a wardrobe, so this was new to him. There were blankets and a pillow and the hammock rocked a little, as if the whole library were out at sea. It gentled and soothed him. After the long, dark day he'd had, the library was singing him a lullaby.

He didn't expect to sleep. So much had happened and was running round in his head. He was wondering where Amanda was. Was she at home or was she in a hospital? Was she thinking of him? And where was Mr Bunting, and was *he* thinking of Rudger too?

But he did sleep, without even noticing it, and the next thing he knew it was morning.

SEVEN

When he woke up, with the electric lights of the library flickering overhead and real people flicking through books either side of his hammock, he climbed down and made his way through the stacks back to the clearing where they'd had the campfire the evening before.

Snowflake wasn't there, but some of the other imaginaries were.

Emily smiled when she saw him. 'Breakfast?'

Cruncher-of-Bones wheeled her squeaking trolley towards him and offered him cakes and another mug of hot chocolate.

There were real people all over the place. One was sitting at the table next to the bouncing ping pong ball, reading a newspaper. The real people simply didn't see the imaginary ones and the imaginaries were ignoring the real ones. It was as if two different worlds had been superimposed on top of each other in the one library. Although they shared the same space, they didn't actually touch.

Or that was what Rudger thought until he put his mug down on top of a book. The book was more on the edge of the table than he'd realised. The hot chocolate unbalanced it and sent it spinning to the floor.

The mug and its contents vanished before they hit the ground, but the book landed with a thud.

The man reading the newspaper looked up.

'We try not to do that, Rudge, me pal,' Emily said, punching him on the arm in a friendly manner. 'It can scare them and we're the good guys, remember?'

Rudger leant down to pick the book up.

'Leave it,' Emily said.

'But…' began Rudger.

'Think about it a moment, Rudge. The bloke's surprised by a book falling off the table. But books do that. Things fall down. It's gravity. He'll go back to his paper in a second and think no more about it. On the other hand, if he sees a book flying up *off* the ground and *onto* the table, that's a different thing altogether. That's just weird and he'll think the place is haunted or something. He'll start having nightmares and it'll all be your fault. And you don't want to do that, do you?'

Rudger shook his head.

'Okay,' she said. 'I've decided, you and me, we're gonna go and befriend a kid this morning. We'll do it together. No point hanging around.'

'But I want to find Amanda,' he said.

'And how you gonna do that?'

'I'll find out where the ambulance took her. I mean, it's obvious isn't it, she's probably in the hospital. I'll go look there.'

Emily shook her head.

'It's as if you've not listened to a word I've said, Rudge. You can't go out there looking by yourself. You leave the library and you'll start to Fade.'

Rudger opened his mouth and held his finger up as if he had thought of something to say.

'What you need to do,' she went on when he didn't say anything other than 'But…', 'is come with me. We'll find you a new friend, and then, when they believe in you, if you still insist, you can try and talk them into a trip to the hospital. But you can't do it alone.'

As much as he wanted to just run out and find Amanda, get his old life back, he knew he had to do what Emily said. She was the one that knew what she was talking about. That didn't stop it feeling awfully frustrating though.

'Come on,' she said, walking towards the notice board.

Emily plucked a likely-looking boy's picture.

'This is the one,' she said. 'I've got a good feeling about him.'

That morning John Jenkins opened his wardrobe door and looked for his coat.

He needed it, since it was raining yet again.

'There you are,' he said as he pulled it out and pulled it on.

As the door shut with a neat little click he had the oddest feeling. It was as if something had crawled across the back of his neck, but on the inside. It said to his brain, 'Something's watching you.'

He hurried from the room, across the landing and started down the stairs. His mum and dad were waiting in the hallway.

'Come on lazybones,' his dad said. 'We'll be late for the film if you don't get on.'

John hurried down, but just as he got to the place on the stairs where he could see across the upstairs carpet, under the chest of drawers on the landing and straight across into his bedroom, he paused for the briefest of moments.

The door to his wardrobe was swinging open.

That was what it had looked like, anyway. But he was sure he'd shut it properly. Hadn't he?

He carried on down the stairs, trying to not look behind him.

'I'll just go check the back door,' his mum said, leaving him and his dad in the hall.

John sat on the bottom step and did his shoes up. He could remember the day, at the start of the holidays, when he first tied the knot by himself. It was most peculiar. Before that he was hopeless, he just couldn't do it. Whichever way his fingers turned and however knot-like the shoelaces had looked, the moment he stood up they'd come undone and his shoes would slip off.

And then one day, without anyone watching him or telling him what to do, when he was just sat on his bed by himself, *abracadabra*, he did it. It was as if he'd always been able to tie knots.

When his mum had expressed her surprise he'd expressed surprise straight back at her. 'Of *course* I can tie my shoelaces,' he'd shouted. 'I'm not a baby!' And he wasn't, he was six years old.

He made the loop round his finger and prepared to pass the other bit of lace through the—

John Jenkins

He stopped.

There'd been a creak on the stairs behind him. Above him.

He and his mum and dad were all downstairs. He had no brothers or sisters. No friend had stayed the night. There was no one up there, but he knew that the only time the second step down from the top of the stairs creaked was when it was trod on. He'd trodden on it many times, he knew the creak like the back of his hand.

He looked at the back of his hand. It was shaking. The knot fell apart.

He didn't look round. He didn't look up the stairs.

'Not done your shoes up yet, John?' his mum said, coming back.

His dad had been reading a letter and hadn't noticed.

'No, Mum,' John said. 'Can you do them for me?'

'Of course, love,' she said, kneeling down in front of him.

'Mum?'

'Yes?'

'Is there…?'

'What?' she said as she tugged his laces tighter than was comfortable.

'Can you look up the stairs?'

'What?' She moved on to the second shoe. She was good at this, fast.

'Is there anyone there?'

'Don't be silly,' she said, still not looking up.

'I… I heard something. The creaky step creaked.'

His mum glanced up.

'Well, there's nothing there now,' she said.

'Did you hear it, Dad? You heard it, didn't you?'

'Sorry? What? No,' was all his dad said, putting the post down and opening the front door. 'Come on, let's vamoose.'

John Jenkins stood up, his shoes nice and tight, his coat nice and warm, but imaginary ice-water dripped down his spine. *Something* was watching him. *Something* was behind him. He could tell, but he couldn't turn round.

He hurried out of the front door as quickly as he could, running in front of his mum and dad and going round the corner to where the car was parked.

As they drove away he finally looked back at the house.

It looked just the same as ever, except...except, he thought he saw, although he couldn't be sure, couldn't swear to it, but he thought, through the rain, that he saw a face at the hall window.

At the hall window of their empty house.

'Well, that went well,' Emily grumbled, throwing herself sulkily onto the settee.

Rudger stood by the lounge door.

'Are you sure you should be sitting there?' he said. 'It's not our house.'

'Oh, don't be such a baby, Rudge. It's our house *now*. We're on assignment. We live here until we're not needed any more.'

'But he didn't see us.'

'Sometimes it takes a while, that's all.'

She's done this before, Rudger thought, *she must know what she's doing.*

Emily folded her arms and then unfolded them, scratched at her cheek and then folded them again. It was like an elaborate dance, just not a very good one.

'We should make another plan,' she said after a moment. 'We need to catch his attention. Just get him to see one of us once, and then we'll be in.'

'How do we do that?' Rudger sat carefully next to her. 'He looked right through us before, in the wardrobe.'

'Yeah,' she murmured to herself. 'If he won't see us when he looks straight on, well, we need to get him to look sideways.'

'Sideways?' Rudger asked.

'Yeah, Rudge, old pal.' Emily was cheering up. She rubbed her hands together as she spoke. 'It's obvious. This one's going to be a *mirror* job.'

The film was so funny that by the time John Jenkins came home, he'd completely forgotten the weird feeling he'd had that morning.

'I'll put the kettle on,' his dad said, after taking his shoes off.

'I'm popping to the loo,' his mum said, nipping up the stairs two at a time.

John was left alone in the hall.

He put a foot on the bottom step and pulled the first of his shoelaces undone. As he did so he glanced up the stairs and suddenly, with a sinking feeling in his stomach, remembered the noise he'd heard earlier on. The fun of the film that had filled him in the cinema sank like a stone in his stomach.

He was looking up the stairs and he couldn't stop looking up the stairs. He had the feeling that if he took his eyes away for a moment something would happen. A door would slam or the stair would creak. If he turned round something would happen. He was petrified, like a rabbit on a country road who can see the lights of the lorry coming and knows nothing other than that he *can't* run.

He swapped feet, lifted the shoe that was still tied up onto the bottom stair.

He reached down, without looking, and tugged at the lace with his fingers. His mum tied good shoelaces, they never got knots and they came apart with one sharp tug.

And then he saw something.

And he jumped.

Literally jumped in the air.

His mum stood at the top of the stairs.

'Oh, sorry, love,' she said. 'Did I scare you?'

'*Mum*,' he moaned.

They sat at the dining table to eat their dinner. It was the last of their family days and his parents liked to do things properly. There was still a week before school started, but this was the last day his mum and dad could both take off work.

What they called the dining room was just a bit of the living room with a dining table in it. If he'd been really good, or if he nagged enough, they'd have the television on and he could watch it from the table at dinner time, but today they were having to talk to one another.

His dad was talking about his bike, how he needed a set of new tyres before the autumn, and his mum was helping herself to salad, when John looked up.

Behind his seat was a Welsh dresser on which his parents put the horrible plates his grandmother bought them every Christmas. On the opposite wall was a big mirror. His dad had bought it at a car boot sale earlier in the summer. He said it would make the room feel bigger. John didn't know if it did, the room had always felt big enough to him, but he liked to look in the mirror when the conversation got dull and the telly wasn't on. He'd look at the back-to-front pictures of kittens on the plates behind him.

There was a kitten sniffing some flowers and there was a kitten sitting on a cushion and there was a kitten with a moustache of cream. Even at six years old and no art expert, John knew his mum was right to think these plates awful. If he'd had a choice as to what plates to have he would have had ones with robots on. Preferably robots breaking things. Preferably robots fighting other robots, and breaking *them*. Maybe if he asked his gran really nicely she'd give them some of *those* plates this Christmas.

And then he stopped thinking about robots because he'd seen something else in the mirror.

He looked at the table in front of him. He looked at his plate with his fish fingers and his peas. And then he looked to his right to where his dad sat. And then he looked opposite him at where his mum was sat. And then he looked to the left. There was an empty place there. A fourth chair that no one sat in. Nobody ever sat in it unless they had a guest. There were only three of them in the family.

'This salad's gone quickly,' his mum said, dropping the last of it onto her plate. 'Did you have some, John?'

John didn't answer her. He looked back up at the mirror.

He looked himself in the eyes and then he looked at his dad and at the back of his mum's head, and then he looked at the fourth chair, the empty one.

There was a teenage girl sat there. She had blonde hair and had a lump of lettuce on the end of her fork. He watched as she shoved it gracelessly into her mouth and he *almost* heard the crunch as she bit down on it.

In the mirror she met John's eye and she winked.

When the neighbours saw John's mum the next morning they asked her about the screaming. She was in the front garden with the estate agent. He was hammering a *For Sale* sign into the lawn. She told the neighbours they'd had some bad news and were all going to stay with her mother for a while.

'Flipping heck,' Emily said, pacing round the Jenkins' front room.

Rudger watched her pacing up and down.

'Is it usually like this?' he asked.

'No,' she barked. 'When you get a kid who *knows what he's doing*, it's a piece of cake. But this Jenkins, he's useless. I mean, what sort of kid makes a noise like that? I've never seen such a scene. Ridiculous.'

'But you scared him, Emily. You gave him a fright.'

'Yeah, but I didn't mean to. Look at me, do I look like a ghost? Is there *anything* scary about me?' She smiled and ruffled her hair. 'I'm not a scary Friend, am I? The boy's obviously, plainly, clearly defective. They should take him back to the shop, get him seen to.'

Rudger waited for her to finish before he said, 'What do we do now?'

Emily slumped on the settee next to him, and lifted her hand up to her face. Was there a slight tinge of transparency to it? How long could the two of them stay out in the real world without a real person to believe in them? Rudger didn't know the answer, and kept *his* hands firmly in his pockets. They tingled.

'There's only one thing we can do,' she said wearily. 'Go back.'

'Finding the door can be tricky,' Emily said. 'It's not just down any old alley, Rudge. You've got to look at it in the right way and it has to want to be seen in the right way. You've got to think it's right for you.'

'Can't we just go in the front door?'

'To the library?'

'Yeah.'

'Well, we could, if we were in the middle of town. But I don't know where we are. All these streets look the same to me. I tell you what. You keep an eye out for a bus to the town centre and I'll look for an alley.'

It took them twenty minutes of walking round the Jenkins' neighbourhood (there were no buses) before they found an alleyway that Emily deemed suitable.

Rudger looked down the alley, a fence-lined passage between gardens. There were some wheelie bins and a broken pushchair a little way down. It smelt sour.

'This one?' he asked.

'Yeah, look at the shadows,' Emily answered.

She pointed to a nearby lamp post and then at the alley.

The shadow of the lamp post went to the right, away from the alley. But the shadow of the fence went the other way. The alley's shadows went the *wrong* way.

'Down there's the door we want, if we want it. But we'd best be quick.'

She held up her hand. It was definitely beginning to Fade. There were thin grey smoky tendrils curling up from her fingertips.

Rudger didn't look at his own hands, but he knew the feeling, as if the softest pins and needles had begun to infest them.

'Excuse me, young lady,' said a voice from behind them. 'Such a dull-weathered day. I'm lost and require assistance finding directions, please.'

Rudger turned round and there on the pavement, moustache bristling, was *that* man.

'Emily,' he said, tugging at her arm, 'don't…'

But Emily wasn't listening. She was stunned. She wasn't used to being seen. She'd been in the imaginary business for long enough to know something odd was going on here. She didn't, however, know exactly what it was.

'Um. How can I help, mate?' she said, pretending to be calm.

'Oh, it's easy,' Mr Bunting said, leaning over her.

Rudger shouted, 'No, Emily, he's Mr Bunt—'

A clammy fish-cold hand clapped across his mouth and tugged him backwards.

It was *her*.

He struggled, trying to bite her fingers, trying to kick her legs out from under her, but it was no good.

Mr Bunting leant over Emily, a hand on her shoulder, and Rudger watched that endless mouth of his open up, unroll, tunnel back into his head. She seemed stuck, like an insect in amber,

unable to move. Rudger assumed she was trying, but she just stood there staring into the dark at the end of his tunnel-throat.

And then she stretched, pulled out like dribbling custard, and with a delicious unlikely slurping noise he swallowed her whole.

Mr Bunting's mouth banged shut with a xylophonous clatter. Grey wisps of smoke leaked out from under his moustache.

He burped a gunpowder burp.

'Oh goodness,' he said, looking happy. 'Now…'

Rudger had been struggling without success. He redoubled his efforts. She might not have been his friend, exactly, but he'd sort of liked Emily. She'd been good to him, in her own way.

He bit harder than he'd ever bitten before and drove his elbow backwards. The dark pale skinny girl fell off him.

Spitting a finger out into the alley's dirt, Rudger ran.

There was a whining hiss like steam escaping a broken pipe and then the clatter of running feet behind him.

He ran as if his life depended on it. Which, had he stopped to think, it probably did.

The alley turned this way and that, the walls changed from wooden fences to red bricks to dark crumbling bricks, dripping and plastered with the torn edges of old posters.

Still the thudding footsteps were behind him.

Mr Bunting and the girl weren't giving up. They weren't *catching* up, since Rudger was fast, but they weren't giving up either.

And Rudger was leading them, he suddenly realised, straight to the Agency, straight to the library. This man who, from what Rudger had seen, ate imaginaries, who liquefied them and swallowed them whole…and Rudger was leading him straight to the one place where he'd find all the off-duty Friends he could ever want.

The thought made him run faster. He just had to get there first.

'I see you, boy,' said a voice Rudger recognised.

Rudger jumped as he ran, and said, 'Kinda busy now, Zinzan.'

The cat sat in a shadow in the middle of the alley, leg up in the air, giving its bum a good, if ineffectual, washing.

And Mr Bunting didn't see it there, not until his foot slammed into it and he flew forwards, falling to the floor in a tumbling, clattering heap.

Zinzan was tough and flexible enough to come out the other side of the collision a little stunned, somewhat topsy-turvy in the mess of the alley, but quite uninjured. Still, climbing to its feet, it realised there was something else to worry about, something it could smell but couldn't see. It wasn't the singed smell of Fading that had passed by with the boy. This was something else, something sickly, like something pickled too long.

Then cold fingers closed around the scruff of its neck and the cat fell numb.

Rudger ran. He heard Mr Bunting trip, heard the screech of the cat kicked, and gave thanks to Zinzan. The smart, fast-thinking cat had saved his bacon.

He turned one final corner and there was the flickering light above the Agency's door.

A second later he had his hand on the handle.

Looking behind him to see if Mr Bunting had got to his feet yet, Rudger was surprised to see a wall. He looked around. He was stood in a little brick-bound courtyard. The alley had sealed itself up, cutting itself off from where he'd just been. It looked as if he was safe at last.

Then he heard a voice say, 'Where's he gone? What a confounding boy it is. Look, look, look. Look at that. All this running and we're back on the street. Madness, imaginary madness.'

It was Mr Bunting talking to himself, or probably, Rudger thought, talking to the girl. He was just the other side of the wall.

This was the brilliance of an imaginary door in an imaginary alleyway. Mr Bunting wouldn't find it now, he couldn't find it on his own and, Rudger really hoped, his girl was unable to work the trick either.

'You're right,' the man said, after listening to his silent companion. 'We must do something about him. I've got an idea where to begin. Remember his little friend...?'

There was a hiss like a wheezing snake and then Rudger heard footsteps going away and finally silence surrounded him and he breathed easy.

He was, at last, once again, safe. *But*, he thought, *poor Emily*. With all the running he hadn't had a chance to really think about what he'd seen. Now he did. She'd been liquefied. Not eaten, but drunk by Mr Bunting. She was gone and he didn't know if there was any way to bring her back.

And then he thought, *Where's the cat?*

And then he thought, I *need to get inside*.

EIGHT

'No, no, no,' Cruncher-of-Bones, the person-sized imaginary teddy bear, said, waving her furry arms in the air to stop Rudger talking. 'There *is* no "Mr Bunting", it's just a story to frighten the recently forgotten with. It's all just an urban myth. We told you last night, remember?'

'No!' Rudger insisted, gabbling, breathless with urgency. 'It's not a myth. It's true. I've seen him again, him and the girl. Just now... looking for the alley... I had to run, but he got Emily. I saw him eat her. There was nothing I could do. I'm so sorry.'

'Who?'

Rudger rubbed his eyes.

'Emily,' he said. 'She's gone, she's—'

'Emily?'

The bear's face was hard to read. Was she playing some sort of game with him, pretending not to have heard the name before? But why?

'I saw him eat her,' Rudger said quietly. 'She's gone, isn't she? She's not coming back.' He paused for a second. 'Or can you? Once he's swallowed you, *is* there a way to come back? Could we rescue her?'

Cruncher-of-Bones rubbed her chin with a paw as if thinking, before saying, 'All the stories I've heard say once you're swallowed you're "lost to the world", as if you never were. That's the phrase they use, "lost to the world". Once you're gone, you're gone. It's worse than Fading.' She stopped and shook her head. 'Or it would be, Rudger, *if* "Mr Bunting" were real, which he's not. He's just made up.' She offered him a cake off her trolley as if the matter were over. 'Maybe a cup of hot chocolate? You like that, don't you?'

'But what about Emily?'

'I don't know what you're talking about.'

It was clear Rudger was going to get nothing out of her. She wasn't playing a game, wasn't pretending. She simply didn't remember Emily. It was as if Emily had been removed from her memory at the same time as she was removed from the world. But Rudger had seen it happen and Rudger still remembered her.

He tried speaking to some of the other Friends.

The bouncing ping pong ball didn't remember her.

A group of a dozen tiny men dressed as gnomes who leapt on him from a bookcase shouting,

'Surprise attack!'

didn't remember her either.

The Friend who looked like an old Victorian schoolmaster, The Great Fandango, requested that Rudger stop wasting his time. He was trying to read a book, he said it was very important, and even though he had it open upside down and had been snoring when Rudger had nudged him, Rudger didn't argue.

Emily had been forgotten by *everyone*.

He wished Snowflake were here. The dinosaur was as big as an elephant and elephants never forget. But maybe even Snowflake would have forgotten Emily.

He'd thought he'd get help at the library, but it looked like he'd been wrong. All he'd found was a roof to hide under and some free food to eat while he tried to come up with a plan of his own to put an end to Mr Bunting's feeding.

Could he do that? Was that really what he wanted to do? Wouldn't he rather just hide away and be safe himself? Wouldn't that be more sensible?

Probably, but Amanda would never have forgiven him.

As he made his way to the hammocks later that night he was stopped by a bark.

He turned to find an imaginary dog behind him.

It was black and white, a shaggy old thing. It looked faint at the edges and grey round the eyes, as if it had seen better days and was now beginning to fray. Rudger remembered seeing it the day before. It was the dog that had been asleep by the notice board.

'Hello,' said Rudger.

The dog barked quietly and cocked its head to one side.

'Can I help you?'

'You're *him*, aren't you?' the dog said, its voice friendly but gruff.

'Him who?'

'The new chap Bones was talking about.'

'I guess so. I'm Rudger.'

'Yes, you're him. So, tell me, Rudger, is it true?' The dog sounded nervous.

At last, Rudger thought, *someone who believes me.*

'Yes, it's all true,' he said.

'Oh, goodness,' the dog said, wagging its tail. 'And…and…how is she, Rudger?'

'You remember her?'

'Of course I do. Of course!'

'Only, no one else round here seems to remember her at all. They act as if they'd never met her, but she was here just this morning.'

'I don't mean to be rude, Rudger, but I don't think she *was* here. I'd've seen her. She's not been in here for years.'

'No, you're wrong. Of course she was. She's the one who showed me round.'

'I don't understand.'

'But now Mr Bunting's eaten her, and no one remembers her, no one but—'

The dog barked, an angry, scared bark.

'What? What?! What do you mean, she's been eaten? Mr Bunting? *The* Mr Bunting?'

'That's what I've been telling everyone.'

'How's that possible? They always said he ate 'maginaries. No one ever mentioned him eating *real* people.'

'But…but Emily wasn't real.'

'Who's Emily?'

Rudger opened his mouth and said nothing. He closed it again. There was *definitely* something wrong with this conversation. He had the sudden feeling there were two conversations going on, side by side.

'Who are you talking about?' he asked the dog.

'Elizabeth Downbeat,' the dog replied, knocking a book off the shelf behind him with a wag of his tail. 'My Lizzie.'

'Oh,' said Rudger. 'Who's she?'

'She was my first friend. She imagined me. Long time ago now. Long ago.'

'But what's this got to do with me?' Rudger asked.

'I heard your friend was my one's daughter.'

'No, there must be some mistake. My…friend…is called Amanda. Amanda Shuffleup.'

'Yes, *your* Amanda is *my* Lizzie's daughter.'

Rudger scratched the dog behind the ear while he took this in.

'All I want to know,' the dog said, 'is…well, is she happy? Did she grow up to be happy?'

'I think so,' Rudger said. 'She's busy with her work at the computer a lot of the time, but she still takes us to the park and swimming, and while the computer's thinking, she makes wonderful cakes. You should smell them! And she laughs at all the things Amanda does, even the stupid things. I see her smile sometimes, when Amanda's not looking. And then when we're supposed to be asleep I sometimes hear her laughing on the telephone, or at the telly. I've not seen many grownups, but I think she's a happy one. I mean she does get a bit annoyed with Amanda *sometimes*. But I don't think she's unhappy. Well, not until—'

'Did she...?' said the dog, interrupting Rudger before he could finish the sentence he was pleased to not have to finish.

'What?'

'Did she ever...mention...me?'

'Um...'

'Fridge.'

'Pardon?'

'My name's Fridge. In case that helps. I mean she probably didn't say, "Oh, I wish that big old imaginary dog of mine was here right now," but you might've heard her say, "I miss Fridge", you know, just sometimes. And you wouldn't have known what it meant, would you?'

The dog had such big pleading eyes that Rudger didn't want to let him down. He racked his brains to try to remember what Amanda's mum *had* said. It was hard, partly because she'd said a lot of things, but partly also because thinking about her made him think of Amanda and of the things he'd love to hear *her* say.

Then he thought of something. 'I don't know if it means anything,' he said, 'but she named a cupboard after you, in her kitchen. The cold one where she keeps the milk.'

'Oh!' said Fridge, the dog.

This seemed to make him happy.

The next morning Rudger stood in front of the notice board and looked at the different faces that were on offer. There were two dozen of them, staring out from their photographs. How should he choose? Which one would be the key to take him home? Which kid would lead Rudger to the hospital, would help him find Amanda? How would it work?

Emily had said, cryptically, 'You just know.'

Fridge was curled up asleep there, as usual, waiting. As Rudger looked at the pictures he heard the old dog yawn.

'Oh, Rudger,' he said. 'Is it morning already?'

'Yep,' said Rudger, a little annoyed at being interrupted in his important task, but also happy to have someone to talk to. 'How do you do this?'

'Choose?' Fridge said.

'Yeah.'

'Don't think too hard.'

Rudger tried not to think.

'Why haven't *you* picked one?' he asked. 'You've been here for ages, Emily said, trying to pick.'

'I'm old, Rudger,' said Fridge, with another yawn. 'I've picked lots. Now I'm just waiting for my last job. One more, then I'll be ready to Fade.'

'Really?'

'Yes. You get tired. I'm wispy round the edges already. I'm thin, you see.'

'I don't mean to be rude, but you're always asleep.'

'I told you, tired.'

'But how will you pick one of these…' Rudger gestured at the pictures '…if you're asleep?'

The dog laughed, a woofish warm chuckle, and nodded his head.

'I'll know,' he said. 'I'll know when it's there.'

He yawned tremendously and walked in a circle several times before lying down.

'Now, if you'll excuse me,' he said. 'You're a good boy, Rudger. I like you.'

And then the dog was asleep again, snuffling snores from under its glistening black nose.

Rudger turned back to the notice board.

As he looked the photographs shifted about in front of one another. They didn't stay still. One would push its way forward, come into better focus, as if it really wanted to be picked, then it would drift back, be replaced by a different photo. It was like watching faces floating on the surface of a sea.

But to Rudger's eyes the children all looked the same: not Amanda.

None of them looked like the next step in his plan.

This was hopeless.

He reached up to grab the nearest picture, to just plump for one of them, any one, when something suddenly, finally, caught his eye.

That girl. That one there. Didn't he know her from somewhere?

Julia Radiche

NINE

That morning Julia Radiche opened her wardrobe door and stared.

'Who are you and what are you doing in my wardrobe?' she said quite calmly, but pulling her dressing gown tight over her pyjamas.

The girl she was looking at, who was about her own height but who had long red hair, curling in ringlets with a bow at the top and freckles on her cheeks, held out her hand and said, 'Hi, I'm Rudger.'

Julia looked at her and snorted.

'Roger?' she said. 'I don't think so. You look like a Veronica to me.'

'Veronica?'

The girl in the wardrobe shook her head and sort of half-smiled, as if Julia were making a joke, even though Julia didn't think she'd made a joke.

'No, I'm Rudger,' the girl repeated. 'I'm Amanda's friend.'

'Amanda's friend?' Julia asked, mulling the words over. 'Amanda?'

'Yes, your friend Amanda.'

Julia stared into the distance for a moment before saying, 'Shuffleup?'

'Yes.'

'Dizzy Shuffleup?'

'No, *Amanda* Shuffleup.'

'You're *her* friend?'

'Yes, but I have met you before. She brought me to school once.'

Julia bit her lip and tilted her head on one side, just the way Amanda did when she was thinking about something. But when Julia did it, it didn't have the same charm. It looked as though she'd practised it in front of a mirror because she thought that was how people looked when they were thinking and she didn't want to be left out.

'Amanda had an *imaginary* friend called *Roger*,' she said eventually. 'She talked about him a few times. But I never—' She stopped and corrected herself. 'Oh, hang on. You're right. She *did* pretend he was there once. Made us all shake hands with him. It was dead funny, we had to try not to laugh. She's weird, that one. Everyone says so.'

The girl in the wardrobe shook her hair out and stomped her foot angrily.

'She's not *weird*,' she snapped. 'Amanda's brilliant, and it's *Rudger*, not *Roger*. And, I'll have you know, you jabbed me in the tummy when you tried to shake my hand.'

'No, that can't be right,' Julia said. 'This Roger of hers was a boy.'

'I *am* a boy!'

Julia coughed the sort of cough you cough when someone's made a silly mistake that it would be rude to point out. She looked the girl up and down, using her eyes like hands to indicate just where the mistake she wasn't going to point out had occurred.

The red-haired girl in the wardrobe looked down at herself, lifted the frills of her skirt, ran a finger through her long curly hair, picked a foot up to look at her pink glittery trainer.

'I'm a *girl*?' she said, staring at Julia. She sounded shocked, surprised, stunned.

'Duh!' said Julia, as if the fact were obvious, which it clearly was.

'But I'm...'

'Veronica,' Julia finished for her. 'And you're *my* new friend.'

Rudger hadn't noticed it happen. You'd've thought, he thought, you'd notice something like that, wouldn't you?

He'd made his way through the library to the Corridor holding Julia's photo, just as he and Emily had done with John Jenkins' picture. He had felt perfectly normal then. He'd pushed through the half-real door and walked down the passage lined with the wallpaper peppered with those small blue flowers. He had felt perfectly normal *then*. He'd pushed through the door at the other end and...

Julia had opened the wardrobe door and found him.

Except she hadn't found *him*.

She'd found *her*.

The answer was simple: Rudger was Julia's imaginary friend now, so he looked the way she wanted him to look. In this case she wanted him to look like a girl called Veronica.

Emily had never warned him this could happen.

Somehow it didn't seem quite fair.

He still *felt* like Rudger inside. He could remember all the Rudgerish things he'd done. He still remembered climbing trees and descending into the bubbling mouths of volcanoes with Amanda, but now his long red hair kept getting in the way of his face and his legs were already getting cold under his skirt.

But Rudger had to face the facts. He'd become a girl.

Julia led Rudger down to breakfast.

'Mum,' she said. 'I want you to meet my new friend.'

'A friend, dear?' her mother said over her shoulder, from the sink where she was doing some washing up.

'Yes, she only arrived this morning, so she's probably hungry.'

'What do you mean, dear? A friend?'

'I found her in the wardrobe. It's okay, she's called Veronica.'

Her mother put a freshly washed mug carefully down on the draining board and turned round.

'Julia, I don't think you should be bringing friends home without telling me beforehand. I've not vacuumed and your father needs to clean the pond out. What would people think?'

'Oh, she doesn't mind. She used to live at Amanda's house and her mum *never* vacuums, everyone knows that.'

Julia's mum stood there for a moment, letting the words her daughter had said sink in. There were quite a lot of words and not all of them belonged together.

'What do you mean, "she used to live at Amanda's house"?' she asked.

'Well, she used to be Amanda's friend Roger, but now she's my friend Veronica.'

'Amanda? Amanda Shuffleup? From your class at school?'

'Yeah,' Julia said. 'But she's too weird so Veronica had to find a new friend, a better one. That's why she came to me. Ow!'

'What happened?'

'Veronica kicked me.'

'She's here?'

'Of course she is. She's stood right there.'

Julia pointed at Rudger.

Her mother looked very carefully at the empty space.

It was definitely space and definitely empty.

'Darling,' she said, slowly.

'What?'

'There's no one there.' (She said this in a tiptoeing half-whisper.)

'Well, *you* can't see her, can you? She's imaginary.'

'Imaginary?'

'Duh!'

Rudger didn't get any breakfast from Julia's mum.

She didn't seem to be as taken with him as Amanda's mum had been. *She'd* always treated him nicely, said 'Good morning' to him whether he was in the room or not. Julia's mother wasn't like that.

While Julia was sat at the breakfast bar eating her breakfast, her mum was in the front room on the telephone.

'I think she's banged her head,' Rudger could hear her saying. 'She's seeing things. I need an appointment urgently. I'm worried it might get worse.'

Rudger, or Veronica, sat on a stool at the breakfast bar next to Julia.

'Julia,' he said.

'What?' she said between mouthfuls of cornflakes.

'Do you know about Amanda?'

'What about her?'

'Do you know she got knocked down?'

'Knocked down?'

'Yes, the other day. It was at the swimming pool.'

'Knocked down? What, by a dog or something?'

'No. By a car. In the car park.'

Julia put her spoon down.

'No way!' she said. 'What an idiot. Who gets knocked down by a car in a car park? They're parked.'

Rudger stared at her for a moment. He couldn't tell if she was making a joke or not. If she *was* making a joke, he didn't think it a very funny one. On the other hand, if she *wasn't* making a joke, then she wasn't being very sensitive.

'No. It was moving,' he said. 'We were running away—'

'I don't want to know,' Julia interrupted, holding her hand up to silence him. Then she leant in closer and added, in a whisper, 'Is she…?'

'No,' said Rudger. 'No, she's not dead. I thought she was, but the cat told me—'

Julia held her hand up again.

'Okay, Veronica,' she said. 'I know you're new here, but I think we should set some rules. For a start, in this house we never begin a sentence with the words, "The cat told me…" Nobody says that. It's mad. I don't want a *weird* imaginary friend who sees talking cats. No way. Secondly, I'm pleased Amanda's not dead, course I am, but can you please stop *going on* about her. You told me you're *my* friend now. If you keep going on about how good everything was with her, then I'll stop believing in you. Understand?'

Rudger was a little taken aback by this. Amanda had always said nice things about Julia, she said they had fun at school together and sometimes swapped sandwiches at lunchtime. But the Julia he was seeing told a very different story.

'I need you,' Rudger said. 'I need you to take me to the hospital. I've got to see her. Amanda.'

Julia folded her arms. She shook her head.

Then she knocked her bowl to the floor.

145

It shattered in a puddle of milk and cornflakes and the spoon rattled across the tiles.

Her mum rushed in, banging through the door.

'Darling? What happened?'

Julia screwed her face up tight and said, 'It was Veronica. She did it.' She pointed at Rudger for good measure.

Rudger was used to being blamed for accidents and for things which weren't *exactly* accidents but which shouldn't have turned out quite how they had. But whenever Amanda dobbed him in she had a twinkle in her eye, she did it with crossed fingers and a wink.

Julia's eyes, on the other hand, twinkled with nothing but malice.

Amanda's mum would listen patiently to her daughter's finger-pointing and tell her to get the dustpan and brush or write a sorry letter to the neighbour and that would be the end of it, but Julia's mum, like Julia, didn't seem to understand exactly how having an imaginary friend worked.

'Oh darling,' she cried, and pulled her daughter to her bosom, patting her back and kissing the top of her head. 'You poor thing. You poor, poor thing.'

The Radiche household seemed, to Rudger's mind, to be a rather highly-strung place, with too much useless emotion sloshing round and about.

And coming here didn't seem to have got him any closer to Amanda. In fact, after the way Julia had spoken to him, he felt further away than ever.

After the breakfast things had been swept up and the milk mopped (by a quiet woman in a pinny who came in two mornings a week to clean) Rudger followed Julia upstairs.

'Today,' she was saying to him, 'is washing day. We have to get all the dirty clothes and clean them.'

'Not the other way round?' Rudger said, trying to make a little joke.

Julia stopped halfway up the stairs and turned to look at him.

'Veronica Sandra Juliet Radiche. You are the most stupid girl I've ever met. *Of course* not the other way round. Who takes clean clothes and makes them dirty? I do wish you'd think before you speak.'

Rudger, who had never dreamt he'd have so many names, did think about it for a moment and said, 'But if nobody ever takes clean clothes and makes them dirty, then why do we have to clean them?'

'Because,' said Julia, in the way that made the one word sound like the end of the conversation. 'Just because,' she added to drive her point home, before turning round and stomping the rest of the way up the stairs.

What surprised Rudger, when he followed, was that instead of emptying a laundry basket and carrying the clothes down to the washing machine, Julia sat down in front of a huge dolls' house and pulled open the walls.

Inside were sat, neatly and upright at tables and in chairs, a dozen dolls of various shapes and sizes.

Amanda had had some dolls, but hers had never looked like this. Julia, it seemed, had never cut her dolls' hair with scissors or glued tin-foil to their faces to make them look more like robots. It seemed such a shame.

'Veronica,' Julia was saying. 'Pay attention. We'll make a pile here,' (she pointed to an area of carpet) 'of the dirty clothes. You start on that side and I'll start here.'

She carefully removed the first doll and began to undress it, laying the clothes out neatly on the bit of carpet she'd indicated.

Rudger sat down next to her, feeling the rough carpet tickling his legs. He shifted himself and tucked his skirt underneath him. If she had to have a girl for a friend, he grumbled to himself, well, he could just about live with that, but why not make him a girl with trousers? How hard would that have been?

He pulled a doll out of the dolls' house by its feet.

'No! No! Be careful,' Julia said, getting flustered. 'Brunhilde doesn't like being upside down. Careful.'

Rudger set her down the right way up. Carefully.

He looked at the dress she was wearing.

'This looks clean,' he said.

'Give it here.'

Julia held out her hand.

Rudger handed her the doll.

Julia looked at it closely, sniffed it and gave it back.

'Dirty,' she said.

After five minutes they had a pile of what Julia called dirty clothes, which to Rudger just looked like clothes, and a dolls' house full of naked dolls.

'Now to wash them!' Julia said, stomping out of her bedroom towards the bathroom.

Rudger followed, a pile of clothes in each hand.

This wasn't the morning he'd hoped for.

On the one hand, he was safe from Mr Bunting. Julia believed in him (well, in Veronica, at least) and he wasn't Fading.

On the other hand, he was no closer to finding Amanda. Julia, who he'd thought would be a direct line to his friend, had turned out to be a dead end. She had no intention of going to the hospital and if *she* didn't go, then Rudger couldn't go either.

He had to come up with a plan. A new plan. An additional plan.

He tried to think while they stood at the bathroom washbasin washing dolls' clothes in soap powder and cold water.

'Mum doesn't like me to use the hot water,' Julia explained when Rudger asked. 'You can burn yourself *and* it wastes electricity.'

How do you get to go to hospital? Rudger thought, as he perched on the toilet lid and hung the miniature clothes on a clothes line that dangled across the bath.

Amanda went there in an ambulance, didn't she? And the ambulance comes when there's an accident.

But Rudger didn't think he could have an accident. Not the sort that would take him to hospital. For a start someone has to see you in order to phone for the ambulance, and for another thing you have to really hurt yourself, and he didn't think he could do that.

He wasn't real, and being hurt was something peculiar to real people, he reckoned. He'd been knocked down at the same time as Amanda, by the same car, but he'd just rolled across the ground and stood up with nothing more than a bruised knee and a scuffed elbow, and even those had vanished before he'd really thought about them.

For an imaginary to get hurt, their real friend would have to imagine them *being* hurt, just like Julia was imagining him in a skirt and with red hair. And that's not the sort of thing friends do.

There was one way though, he thought. A plan had just popped into his head. It was dangerous, it could go terribly wrong, but if it worked, if it didn't backfire on him, then it would get him to the hospital.

But could he do it? Did he dare? Should he? It was exactly the sort of thing friends shouldn't do to one another, but he felt he had no other choice.

'Julia?' Julia's mum shouted up the stairs.

'Yes?' Julia shouted back.

'Is…um…is Veronica still there?'

'Yes, Mum. We're in the bathroom.'

'Um…what are you doing, darling?'

'What do you think we're doing?' Julia shouted with a sneer. 'I said, "We're in the bathroom."'

Her mum went away.

Rudger looked at his plan again. He looked at the row of little dolls' clothes dripping into the bath and then he looked at Julia. This was what she did for fun, he told himself. The sooner he got back to Amanda the happier they'd all be. It was the only way.

'What are we doing now?' he asked. Julia thought for a second, drying her hands on a towel.

'A glass of squash, I think. After all this hard work.'

She walked out onto the landing. Rudger followed.

He looked his plan in the eye one last time, hoped he was doing the right thing and said, 'Sorry,' under his breath.

As Julia got to the top of the stairs, he hooked one of his feet round her ankle, gave her shoulders a shove with his hands and sent her flying.

TEN

Julia tripped at the top of the stairs and plunged forwards into empty air.

'Arrgghhh!' she shouted as she fell.

At that moment, as if luck were on her side, her mother walked into the hallway, phone in hand, saying, 'Darling, put your shoes on, I've—'

Faced by the sudden surprising sight of her daughter plummeting towards her, she dropped the phone and instinctively flung her arms out.

Julia landed on top of her and the pair of them fell backwards, not falling over, but banging into the front door.

'What happened? Are you okay?' her mum asked when she got her breath back.

'Veronica tripped me,' Julia said, almost in tears.

'That's it,' her mum said calmly, but firmly. 'I was just saying, I've managed to get you an appointment with a special sort of doctor.'

'A doctor? I'm not ill. I don't need a doctor.'

'Oh, darling,' her mum said, stroking a strand of hair away from Julia's face. 'You don't know what you're saying. If you're still seeing this Veronica, if you really think she tripped you up just now, then I'm afraid you're going to *have* to see him.'

'I hate doctors,' Julia said, pushing herself away from her mum. 'They smell funny and have cold hands.'

Her mum picked her phone up.

'Nevertheless, darling, we've got an appointment at the hospital in forty-five minutes.'

'But...'

'Put your shoes on.'

At the top of the stairs Rudger felt awful.

As soon as he'd hooked his foot round her ankle he realised that his plan was *wrong*, but it was too late then to stop his hands from pushing her. The plan wasn't wrong in the sense that it might not work, but wrong in the sense that it made him feel bad inside.

As much as he needed to get to the hospital to find Amanda, he shouldn't have to hurt someone else to get there. What would

Amanda have said about it? She'd've been mad at him. Julia was her friend, and she'd be upset if Rudger hurt her.

He was just thankful that Julia's mum had appeared when she had. It made him feel slightly better.

Then he heard what her mum had said. She was taking Julia to the hospital. This was it. This was the chance he'd been looking for. It had worked after all!

He watched Julia dragging her heels as her mum opened the front door.

'Mum,' she complained.

He crept downstairs.

Julia saw and gave him a dirty look. 'You tripped me,' she said.

Her mum pushed the door to and whispered, 'Is she still here, darling?'

'She's on the stairs. I think she wants to come with us.'

'Oh,' her mum said. 'I suppose the doctor might want to see her too.'

'No,' Julia said, gritting her teeth and turning away. 'She can stay here. I *hate* her.'

Rudger felt the faintest of tingles in his left foot as she said the words. He recognised it. He'd felt it before. It was the first hint of the sort of faint tingle that came before you started Fading.

He really wasn't very good at this 'being an imaginary friend' business, he thought.

He'd messed it all up. Entirely.

Julia slammed the door behind her before Rudger could get through it.

He pulled at the handle, but Julia's mum had locked it from the outside. He was trapped indoors.

He ran through the living room to the kitchen. There was a back door there. He'd seen it when they'd had breakfast, but when he tried the handle he found it was locked too.

The windows?

He'd have to climb up onto the work surface and then move that vase of flowers out of the way, but, never mind all that, they looked like the sort of windows that locked anyway and he didn't know where the key was.

It wasn't worth wasting time trying to look for it. Julia and her mum would probably be in the car by now and in a minute they'd be on their way.

He looked around. He'd come so close. Finally someone was going to the hospital, but it wasn't him. He could've screamed with frustration. Instead, he kicked the stool he'd sat on at breakfast.

It fell over and rolled across the floor.

Rudger looked at where it had ended up, next to the back door and he noticed something he hadn't seen when he was trying the handle.

There was a cat flap.

He knelt down and pushed his head through.

The flap was unlocked, which was a good thing, and his head was out in the fresh air of the garden, but his shoulders wouldn't go through.

Somewhere nearby he heard the sound of an engine starting up, a car's engine turning over.

Then there was that tingle in his feet, that tingle in his hands. If he was being ignored, being *unbelieved* by Julia, maybe he could use it to his advantage. He thought of Amanda, tried to remember what the feeling had been like before he had met Zinzan, when he had believed she'd gone and left him alone in the world. How soft, how wispy he'd felt then.

He had to think she was dead, had to believe Julia hated him. He tried to remember Emily, how she'd gone too, but found he couldn't quite remember what she'd looked like. She was Fading in his memory, just like she had in everyone else's.

There was a smell of gunpowder in the air, the whiff you get from firing a cap gun ten times in a row, but no one had been shot.

Rudger was Fading.

He twisted and pushed and his shoulders grew soft.

The plastic rim of the cat flap felt like sand, like dust, and with a sudden *fluff* he slipped through, out into the garden.

Hitting the ground didn't hurt.

He picked himself up. He felt so sad. His heart ached. He just wanted to sit down and let it all go, but then he heard the

sound of wheels on gravel, the noise of a car moving off, and he remembered what he was doing this for.

He stood up straight, the crazy paving beneath his feet grew hard again, and he ran. He pulled the gate open and sprinted through.

There was Julia's car, reversing away from him. He could see her mother looking over her shoulder, watching where she was going, and he could see Julia in the back seat pointing at him. She was saying something he couldn't make out.

There was no way, he realised, Julia was going to let him in the car, so he did the only thing he could think of.

He ran at it, leapt up onto the bonnet and grabbed hold of the windscreen wipers.

Julia's mother couldn't see him, of course, so he wasn't blocking her view of the road, but Julia could. She was pointing and shouting from the back seat.

Rudger couldn't make out the words.

He knew one thing though. While he clung there on the bonnet, straight in front of her, there was no way Julia could *not* believe in him. He felt more real than he had all day: the hot metal under his chest, the cool glass against his knuckles.

And then they drove off, and the wind, which had been of no concern, suddenly became of no small concern.

Rudger had never ridden on the bonnet of a car before, and he had never worn a skirt before either. Amanda always encouraged him to be open to new experiences and this morning he was getting two of them.

The wind whipped his skirt up over his head, like a blanket covering the whole windscreen, exposing his legs, and whatever knickers Julia had imagined for him, to the whole world. Thank goodness, he thought, for not being real. (And thank goodness she'd imagined him having any knickers at all.) This could have been *incredibly* embarrassing, instead of just, as it was, *very* embarrassing.

To Julia, who was watching from inside the car, the sight of the entire windscreen covered by Veronica's skirt was a bizarrely confusing and worrying experience. On the one hand, she could imagine what the other side looked like, and that was quite funny, but on the other hand, the *entire windscreen* was covered up with a skirt and her mother was still driving.

Julia didn't know how to drive, but she had a feeling that being able to see where you were going was one of the things that drivers like.

'Mummy,' she said, anxiety leaking into her voice.

'Yes, darling?' her mum said.

'She's still there.'

'On the bonnet, darling?' Her mum sounded calm. Eerily so.

'Yeah. Put the windscreen wipers on.'

'But it's not raining.'

'Just do it.'

Julia's mother, unsure what else to do with a daughter growing ever more hysterical in the back of the car, flicked the switch that started the wipers wiping.

Rudger clung on.

Eventually the car pulled up in the hospital car park.

'Now, darling,' Julia's mum said as they climbed out of the car. 'We've got to look for a sign that says "Child Psychologist". Can you help me look?'

They walked off toward the huge building. Its hundreds of windows glinted in the sunshine like an illuminated cliff-face.

Julia looked back at the car one last time and gave a wicked little laugh.

By the time they'd come to a stop Rudger was sore all over and very cold up the skirt. The whole thing would've been easier to cope with in trousers. Amanda would definitely have given him trousers, he thought, every time. (Although, thinking that, he realised that, had Amanda known Rudger *could* travel on the bonnet of the car, she would've made him do it by now, just for fun. He made a mental note to never mention it to her, just in case.)

Once Julia and her mum had gone he slid himself off the bonnet.

He wobbled like a boy who's just got off a runaway roundabout, or been through a washing machine.

He caught a glimpse of himself in the car's wing mirror and saw the strange red-haired girl he'd become staring back at him.

When the world had finally stopped doing its impression of a rolling South Atlantic seascape, he stood up straight and walked towards the hospital.

ELEVEN

Rudger had to keep brushing his hair out of his eyes and pushing his tatty skirt down at each sharp gust of wind. He'd had no practice dressing like this. It took getting used to.

He wondered how long it would last; whether, now Julia had disowned him, he'd change back to normal, or whether he'd be stuck this way forever. Or rather, until he Faded. The tingle had returned.

His first task was to find Amanda. That would be the answer, surely? She'd imagine him back the way he *should* be.

Rudger walked up to the glass doors at the entrance to the hospital. They slid apart as he approached. That was very welcoming. Very friendly. After all he'd been through, a little friendliness really lifted his spirits.

He walked into the reception area.

There was a counter with a sign saying *Information* hanging above it. They'd be able to tell him where Amanda was, except…

Except he was imaginary. The person sat behind the desk couldn't see him.

But that was easy, wasn't it? All he had to do was sneak behind the counter and find a list of rooms or something. How hard could that be?

In a moment he was stood behind the receptionist, looking over his shoulder at folders full of bits of paper. They didn't seem to be any help. The hospital was a big place, the lists went on for page after page and Rudger didn't understand what all the abbreviations and numbers next to people's names meant.

This was worse than useless.

Maybe if he found a sign to the children's ward (they'd put all the children together, wouldn't they?) then he could just search bed by bed. Maybe that would be best.

As he thought that thought he happened to look up.

The automatic doors were sliding open and a man was coming in. Rudger recognised him in an instant. It was the way he ran his hand through his moustache. It was the way he slid his dark glasses up onto the top of his bald head. It was the way he looked exactly like Mr Bunting.

It was Mr Bunting.

Rudger crouched down and ten seconds later heard his voice addressing the receptionist.

'Shuffleup? Does it have a room?'

'Shuffleup? Do you have a first name?'

'Me?'

'No, the patient. Common name, you know?'

'Oh. I see. Yes, of course. It's called…*Amanda* Shuffleup.'

'Let me see.'

The receptionist ran his finger down several sheets of paper before he found what he was looking for.

'Fourth floor,' he said. 'Room 117. But visiting hours aren't until after lunch. It's family only in the mornings. Or…are you family?'

'No,' Mr Bunting said, shaking his head. 'I'm not family. Just a family friend. This afternoon, you say? 117?'

'Two o'clock onwards.'

'Very good. I'll wait.'

'Okay,' the receptionist said, looking down at his paperwork.

After a few seconds he looked up again.

'Is there something else I can help with?' he said.

'Smell?' Mr Bunting said, sniffing. 'I smell something. Can you smell something?'

'Oh, that's the new cleaners,' the receptionist said. 'They only started on Monday and I've told them not to use the lemon fresh stuff. Some people are allergic, aren't they? Peanuts and the like. I mean, this is a hospital, isn't it?'

'Mmm,' said Mr Bunting, ignoring the receptionist and talking to himself now. 'Not lemons. It's…nothing.'

After another moment he walked away. Rudger heard the heavy footsteps retreating. There was a biro on the floor by the receptionist's foot. He picked it up and wrote, '4' and '117' on the back of his hand. Mr Bunting had been helpful.

But why was *he* looking for Amanda?

And what had he smelt? Was it Rudger? They'd said he could smell Fading. That's how he'd got what's-her-name the other day.

Rudger peeked round the edge of the information desk. Mr Bunting was sat on a bench by the doors looking through a newspaper.

Rudger ran, as quietly as he could, over to a door labelled *Stairs*.

Rudger walked past doors that opened onto colourful wards full of poorly kids and past rooms filled with beeping machines and grim-faced grownups.

In one room a little girl sat on a chair by a bed. She looked up and saw him looking at her. She smiled.

Rudger smiled back.

He almost went in to talk to her, to say something like, 'Look out for yourself. There's a man downstairs in the lobby who eats people like me and you,' but he didn't want to worry her. Mr Bunting was here for Amanda and that meant, Rudger knew, that Mr Bunting was actually looking for *him*. He hoped it meant the others were safe for now.

He smiled at the girl again and looked at the room number: 84.

He carried on up the corridor.

It was long and smelt of cleaning chemicals and bandages. Porters pushed trolleys into lifts and a cleaner lazily mopped along the skirting board. None of them saw him.

Still, he had the oddest feeling he was being watched.

He looked behind him.

There was no one there. The little girl hadn't come out of her room to look at him. No one was looking at him. The only people he could see were all real.

But still, as he walked down the corridor the oddest feeling tickled at the back of his neck.

He counted the doors on either side, watching the numbers grow bigger.

Round a corner and there was a storeroom on the left labelled 109. He hurried on and, four doors down, there was 117.

Rudger opened the door. Amanda's mum looked up as he came in.

'That door again,' she said, getting up and shutting it behind him.

Amanda was lying in the bed, a small shape under the blankets. There were machines to one side that had little red lights that blinked on and off. Her head was bandaged where she'd hit it and her left arm was in plaster. It must have been broken. Rudger remembered how strangely twisted it had looked when he'd last seen her.

She was sleeping.

He couldn't tell if his heart had stopped or was beating so fast he couldn't feel the beats, just a hum like a hummingbird caught in his chest. He was light-headed. Here was Amanda. Here he was and here was Amanda. After days apart, they were together again.

Rudger wept. (Just one tear. Any more and Amanda would take the mickey.)

There was a magazine on the chair by the bed. Amanda's mum picked it up as she sat back down. She held it flat on her lap but didn't look at it.

There was a little washbasin on one wall and a large cupboard next to it with a label saying, *For patient use only.*

They were deep inside the hospital here and the room had no windows, only a poster with a picture of a sunny forest scene pinned up beside the wardrobe. It wasn't the prettiest of rooms, but it had Amanda in it.

Rudger stood at the foot of her bed and looked at her.

She looked peaceful. The noise of her breathing was the same as the noise she made at night, in her own bed. It reminded him of being in his wardrobe at home. He wished he could ask her mum (Fridge's Lizzie, he thought with a smile) how she was. He longed to know exactly what had happened.

At the foot of the bed, hanging on the metal frame, was a clipboard with notes on, but it wasn't this that caught Rudger's eye. Instead it was the slender sapling growing from the bed-frame's corner, like a single post of a four-poster bed. It grew straight up,

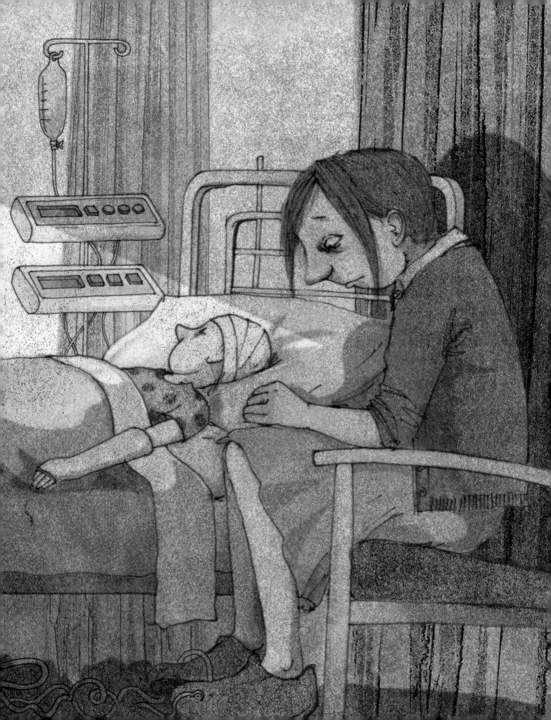

only a metre or so into the air, but it had a couple of thin branches coming off it with a few leaves growing on each of them.

Importantly, it wasn't real.

Even while she slept, Amanda's imagination was making her room her own.

Rudger was proud of her. This was why he wanted to be *her* friend, not John Jenkins' or Julia's, but Amanda's, because *she* had a real gift.

'Amanda, darling,' Amanda's mum said to her sleeping daughter. 'I'm going to get a cup of tea. You stay there. I won't be long. Do you want anything from the café?'

Amanda said nothing.

Her mum smiled a thin smile as if Amanda had said, 'No thanks, Mum.'

She looked ever so tired, Rudger thought. There were dark bags under her eyes and her hair wasn't as neat as it usually was. It looked like she'd been here at the hospital all night. He wondered who was at home looking after Oven, the cat.

She went out.

Rudger dropped her magazine on the floor and sat in the chair. It was warm. He put a hand on the white sheet of the bed by Amanda's shoulder, and brushed his long red hair out of his face with the other.

'Amanda,' he said. 'It's me, Rudger.'

He said it quietly, so as to not wake her. Which was silly, because he wanted to wake her, just for a moment, just to let her know he was there, that he'd come all this way and that he'd found her at last. Then she could sleep for as long as she wanted.

He prodded her softly.

'Amanda?'

Had she stirred? Had her breathing changed? Had her eyelid flickered?

He leant over, leant on the bed and put his lips right up next to her ear.

'Amanda,' he said, squeezing her hand gently. 'I'm so sorry I got you hurt. It was all my fault. If you hadn't imagined me, Mr Bunting would never have chased us and you…you wouldn't have got knocked down. It's my fault. All my fault. I'm so sorry. Wake up soon. I miss you.'

It felt good to have said all that. It was a weight off his shoulders, though he'd have to say it again when she was actually listening.

He sat back in the chair and looked around the room.

One corner was darker than all the others.

It looked odd.

And then there was a flicker and a crackle and the lights went out.

TWELVE

Although the lights in Amanda's room had gone out, there was still a shaft of light shining through the window in the door.

Rudger saw the girl, the dark-haired silent girl, Mr Bunting's ice-fingered friend, as she stepped out of her cloak of shadows into the rectangle of light.

He was on his feet in an instant, leaping to the foot of the bed, putting himself between Amanda and the girl, which was both brave and foolish, he realised, since it wasn't Amanda she was here for, but he didn't care.

The girl tilted her head to one side with a bony clicking sound and stared at him as if she didn't know who or what he was. He was, he remembered, dressed as a girl himself, all in pink.

She sniffed twice, then lowered her head and nodded. He *was* what she'd been waiting for after all.

What was Rudger to do?

'Amanda!' he shouted. 'Amanda, wake up!'

There was no movement behind him.

And then the girl pounced, fingers out like talons (even the finger he'd bitten off in the alley was there, he noticed, stunted, stubby, but already re-nailed like a claw), and she was on him, hissing and grasping and struggling with him, and all the time staring her blank-eyed stare.

He banged back against the bed, her cold hands gripping him.

Hospital beds have wheels and someone had obviously left the brakes off on Amanda's. Each time they knocked into it, as they struggled, it rolled backwards and bumped against the wall.

Anyone in the corridor outside would have seen a bed banging itself against a wall, in the half-dark. *No wonder people believe in ghosts*, Rudger thought. But ghosts were of no use to him. What he really needed was help, and help wasn't coming.

He knew what *was* coming though, what *must* be coming, what was almost certainly on its way up the stairs even now, never mind visiting hours and hospital rules: something big, something bald and something hungry.

The bed banged a third time against the wall and there was a groan from behind him. A small one. Then a cough and a moan.

'Oh,' groaned Amanda in a small, sleepy voice.

'Amanda!' Rudger shouted, a sudden bubble of hope bobbing up inside him.

The girl, clutching him coldly, hands like knots of seaweed, hissed in his face. Her breath was dead. It was death.

He twisted enough to see the outline of Amanda sitting up in bed. She was touching her bandaged head with her good arm.

'Amanda, help!' he cried, between breaths.

But she didn't hear him. She didn't see him. She didn't see either of them.

With one hand he gripped the slender sapling, and heaved himself up so his backside was resting on the frame of the metal bedstead. He was able to lift his feet up and get them against the girl's chest. With all his strength he half-pushed, half-kicked her off him, knocking the clipboard to the floor in the process.

Amanda yawned.

Where was she? She looked around blearily and yawned again.

It didn't look like her bedroom. It didn't smell like home. She'd been having the strangest dreams.

Then the bed rocked. There was a clatter as something fell to the floor.

This wasn't normal.

She felt light-headed and groggy, she ached all over, was thirsty, hungry and ever so tired, but when the bed shook again she blinked away some of the sleep, pushed the pain to one side and sat up straight.

She looked around.

She guessed she was in a hospital. Her left arm was in a plaster cast and throbbed dully. Her mum's coat was draped on the back of the chair by her bed. Her head ached terribly. She'd been in an accident of some sort. She remembered running and there being a car. A hospital was the right place to wake up.

None of that surprised her. But there was a tree growing from the foot of the bed. A sapling, she thought. And it was wobbling. That was odd. The way it wobbled like that, as if it had been caught in a breeze, was weird because there was no breeze.

It was a pretty tree, she thought, and as she watched it grew taller, pushing aside ceiling tiles and letting daylight into the room.

She felt better with the addition of a little light and wondered where her mum was.

And then the door opened.

Mr Bunting shut the door behind him.

As he glanced at the imaginary tree he sneered and it withered. The leaves shrivelled on the branches and the branches wizened and drooped.

'You're awake, little girl,' he said, his moustache fluffling with each word. He looked round the room. 'But not, I think, *awake*.'

'Who are you?' Amanda asked. 'Are you a doctor?'

'No!' Rudger shouted. 'He's not a doctor!'

He was still struggling with the girl. She'd twisted around and managed to bend one of his arms up behind his back. She'd wound his long red hair tight in her other fist. The fight was more or less over. He was caught.

She pulled him backwards, into the middle of the room, and offered him to Mr Bunting like a cat offers a twitching bird to its owner.

The man held out his hand and touched Rudger's cheek.

'Are you sure this is him?' he asked.

A putrid hiss escaped the girl's lips.

'I see. Well, Rudger the Pink, you've been a nuisance. Given us a right run around and about, haven't you? See this?' He pointed to a graze on his forehead. 'Falling over your badly-mannered stinking cat, that was. You *hurt* me, little Rudger. But, my dear little pink-frocked friend, even luck has a date of expiration, and guess what? Yours is today.'

Rudger knew what would happen next, he wanted to run, to fight free and leap away, but the girl had him frozen to the spot.

'No,' he said.

It took most of his strength to say the single word. The girl's ghoulish grip had drained all his energy. He was beaten. Finally done for. For good.

'Who are you talking to?' Amanda asked. 'Who's Roger? What's that hissing?'

The man who she had thought at first was a doctor but who she now thought probably wasn't (mainly because he was stood in the middle of the room talking to himself) turned to look at her.

'Oh, look at that,' he said, from under his moustache. 'She can't see you.'

Even though he looked into her eyes as he said it, she had the distinct feeling he wasn't talking to her. Her head ached. There was something wrong.

He turned away and went on. 'She doesn't remember you, Rudger. A bang on the head can do that. So sad. Worth a tear perhaps? Sweeten the flavour. I'd best have you before you Fade. Think of me as a friend, kind Mr Bunting doing a Friend a favour.'

She *had* had a bang on the head, he was right, and she knew that made people lose their memories. It was called amnesia. She remembered that. But what was it she had forgotten? He was right. There *was* a hole there somewhere. She waggled the tongue of her memory in the space of it. A definite hole.

But what it was that was missing, she couldn't say.

The room was in half-darkness, the sapling had died, the ceiling tiles had fallen back into place. She was feeling sick and tired. Ever so tired.

She lay back down on her pillows. It would be easier to sleep, wouldn't it? She needed her rest, didn't she? That's what they always said on the telly, wasn't it?

So tired, she felt her eyes falling shut under their own weight.

'Amanda!' Rudger shouted again, summoning the strength to speak from deep in his despair, his panic and anger. 'Help me!'

She'd slumped back on to the big white pillows.

The fact that she could see Mr Bunting but couldn't see *him* was like salt on a grazed knee. It was an insult. It stung. She was *his* friend, not Mr Bunting's. If she saw anyone it ought to have been him.

It was unfair, it was unkind, and it hurt him inside.

With Mr Bunting looming, and the distant desert smell of rotting spices edging into the room, Rudger put the very last of his energy into one more struggle.

He bucked and the girl stumbled. Her grip didn't loosen, her hand was still tangled up tight in his hair, but at least he'd made her stumble.

They toppled backwards and banged against the cupboard marked For patient use only.

With a retching gurgling hiss the girl lurched upright and shoved Rudger forwards again, in front of her, until they were stood exactly where they'd been before.

Amanda heard a bang from the cupboard and pushed herself up on her elbows to look. She saw the cupboard rock back against the wall.

And then its door swung open.

The light from the hallway outside lit the inside of the wardrobe.

She saw her coat and a pair of jeans hanging on a hanger and her rucksack on the floor. It was all her stuff. All waiting for her.

On the inside of the wardrobe door was a full-length mirror. One day, when she was better, she'd put her own clothes back on, and she'd look at herself in the mirror, and—

Oh, she thought, as the previous thoughts all fell silent.

The door was swinging to and fro and the mirror was reflecting something *different* to what she could see in the room.

There was a girl dressed in pink struggling in the arms of some pale monster. A skeleton-shape wrapped in a thin shifting cover of moonlit flesh and skin. Long black hair ragged and split and cobwebbed.

The sight jogged something inside her, a memory, a memory, a memory…of being in her mum's study. She remembered hiding under the desk, remembered Goldie, the babysitter, looking for her.

What was *that* all about?

And who was the girl struggling with the ghoul?

And why did Amanda want to think the word 'boy' instead of 'girl'?

And then it came back to her.

All of it.

THIRTEEN

Rudger felt a shudder go through him, a weird warming shiver, and then something happened.

He was free.

Although the girl had loosened her grip on his arm when they'd fallen, she'd twisted his long red hair tighter in her other hand. But now that long hair was gone. She had been left clutching mist as Veronica had vanished and he'd become the real imaginary Rudger.

Forgotten energy surged in his limbs, his heart beat free, and he seized the moment. He pushed away from her, ducked past Mr Bunting and ran for Amanda's bed.

Free of the girl, he felt hope surge back into him. They had a chance.

'Quick,' Amanda said, holding out her good hand and pulling him up onto the mattress.

'Oh dear, oh dear, oh dear,' Mr Bunting said, turning round slowly to face them and shaking his head. 'I had hoped to not have to…upset…young Miss Shuffleup. Forgetting is quite natural, my dear, and hurts so much less. When I take him now—'

'You're not going to take Rudger,' Amanda said, interrupting him.

'He eats imaginaries,' Rudger whispered. 'I've seen him do it.'

'We've got to get out of here,' Amanda whispered back.

'How?'

They looked around. It did seem, at first sight, an impossible task. Not only was Amanda still weak and injured (though feeling brighter, more awake now she had Rudger by her side), but the only way out was through the door behind Mr Bunting and he wasn't going to let them go. It looked an impossible task at second sight too.

There was a high hissing noise and the dark-haired girl leapt at them. She didn't look like the monster Amanda had seen in the mirror, just the sad pale girl she'd seen once on the doorstep, but even that was frightening enough.

Rudger shrank back, remembering the touch of her hands, but before she landed on the bed something happened.

There was a shimmer in the air.

Instead of landing on top of them, the girl crashed onto the glass dome that had appeared from nowhere and now covered the bed.

Rudger looked around. At his side was a control panel, a bank of brass buttons and gauges and handles. He recognised it. He remembered it. Of course he did. It was the submarine they explored the oceans in.

But that had been imaginary. It hadn't been real.

He looked at Amanda.

'First thing that came to mind,' she said. 'If it keeps the water out, it might keep *them* out.'

'But it's not real,' Rudger said.

'And I don't reckon they are neither,' said Amanda.

The girl above them was scratching at the thick, impervious glass, her face white with anger, her eyes motionless dark pits. Her hair floated around her, like a black dandelion, wafted back and forth by underwater currents.

'She'll never get in,' Amanda said. 'I built this thing to last.'

The girl stopped scratching at the dome. She sat up, sat still and looked away. She looked at Mr Bunting.

He was clapping. He had on a diving suit, one of those old-fashioned ones with the big brass helmet and the little round glass windows. Fish swam past him.

'Very clever it is,' he said. His voice crackled as it played through their cabin's speakers. 'A girl with bright sparks. A girl with big dreams.'

Amanda pressed the intercom button and said, 'Not with *dreams*. With a two-person submersible capable of staying submerged for up to eight hours at depths of greater than three miles. You'll just have to wait.' She took her finger off the button and whispered to Rudger, 'By then Mum *must've* come back and she'll get a security guard or something. Chuck him out.'

'You forget one thing, little girl,' Mr Bunting said.

'Yeah?'

'I'm so much *older* than you. So much cleverer, bigger, wiser. I have seen so many more things. I have dreamt of so much. I have imagined worlds that you couldn't even think names up for. I have travelled and eaten in every—'

The girl, perched on top of the submarine's dome, banged on the glass and hissed bubbles at him.

'Yes, yes,' Mr Bunting said, waving his hand dismissively. 'Too long and perambulatory a speech, I know, I know. But, at least, please, let me just say this. You, girl…' He raised a hand and slowly pointed at Amanda. '…are in my way.'

His moustache ruffled inside the brass helmet and in the blink of an eye both the ocean and the submarine, controls, glass dome and all, vanished. In their place Amanda and Rudger found themselves lying, suddenly and unexpectedly, in a bed of writhing, wriggling, coiling snakes. But before they could scream about that, the girl fell on top of them.

As she fell she turned like a cat, twisting in the air so she landed with her hands already gripping Rudger's wrists and her knees pinning his legs to the bed. She was dripping wet.

Before Amanda could move warm ropes of snake curled round and across her arms and legs and waist and neck. She was caught.

'You're not the only one with an imagination, little girl.' Mr Bunting chuckled sourly. 'Now, I'm hungry. I've been hungry for hours and I need to . . . *borrow* your friend, if you don't mind. Bring him here.'

The girl dragged Rudger off the snake-bed, pulled him back into the middle of the room, wrenched him into an upright position.

There was nothing he could do. He felt so tired, and the cold grip of her fingers dripped despair into his brain. He could hardly be bothered to struggle at all.

Amanda was no better off. She was trapped in her bed by snakes and, although she wasn't especially scared of snakes, the experience was not thrilling her. She tried imagining herself free. She tried imagining Rudger free. She tried imagining anything, but it was too hard. The snakes filled too much of her mind up, the way they squeezed, the way they writhed around her. It ruined her concentration.

All she could do was watch.

'At last,' Mr Bunting said. 'You got away too often, you did. It was fun, yes. A challenge. Better than most. But in the end, boy, it changes nothing.'

Mr Bunting stopped talking and unhinged his jaw. That tooth-tiled, unnatural, *supernatural* tunnel-throat unfolded into his head

and beyond, back to wherever its dark-eyed ending was. The scent of rotting spice, of hot dust and sand, hit Rudger in the face and he *tried* to get a hand free, *tried* to get loose, *tried* to make one last weak attempt to get away.

But his world tipped up and Mr Bunting's throat was suddenly beneath him, a tiled pit, a white well with that far speck of absolute darkness at the bottom of it.

He felt himself falling, he was beginning to go, and then, unexpectedly, a voice he knew interrupted it all and the lights crackled and came back on and Mr Bunting's mouth snapped shut with a clanging, clattering *boom*.

'Excuse me?' Amanda's mum said.

She had a cup of coffee in one hand, with a plastic-wrapped cake balanced on top of it. She'd used her other hand to open the door and was just shutting it with her bum when she saw Mr Bunting.

'What are you doing in my daughter's room?' she asked. 'Can I help you?'

She wasn't worried exactly, more curious. There was probably a perfectly simple explanation. This was a hospital, after all, and there were people in and out of rooms all the time. Except he didn't look like one of the nurses or the cleaners, they all had uniforms, and he wasn't the doctor who'd examined Amanda before.

And then she realised that she recognised him. But where had she seen him before? That bright Hawaiian shirt? Those Bermuda shorts? That bald head? Oh, she *did* know him, she thought, but couldn't think where from.

'Ah, Mrs Shuffleup,' he began. 'I'm just in the hospital conducting a survey.'

'In my daughter's room?'

'I was looking for you.'

'You came to the house the other day,' Mrs Shuffleup said, finally remembering him. 'How did you know I was here?'

'What a good memory it has,' he said.

Mrs Shuffleup recalled the odd feeling she'd had then. She was having it again now.

'I think I'd like you to leave,' she said firmly.

'There's nothing to worry about,' he said, in his smoothest tone of voice. 'Don't you believe me?'

'Mum!' croaked Amanda.

She'd been struggling with the snakes more than ever since her mum had come back, but one had slithered right across her mouth, silencing her. By biting and blowing, though, and by tickling it with her tongue, she'd managed, finally, to get it to wriggle out of the way.

'Mum!' she croaked again. Her voice was weak, little more than a whisper. The snake across her throat was wound round tight.

'Amanda,' her mum stuttered with shock. 'You're awake! Oh, my darling.'

She ran over to the bedside, sat down in the chair and stroked Amanda's forehead. She didn't see the snakes.

'You're so hot,' she said. 'But you're awake, at last. Darling, I had hoped and hoped. Oh, I wish I'd been here for you when you—'

'Don't believe him, Mum,' Amanda whispered, interrupting her. 'He's got Rudger.'

'Rudger?'

'He's going to eat him.'

'Oh, that's such a *mean* thing to say, little girl,' Mr Bunting said. '*Eating* isn't the right word at all. I'm going to *borrow* him. *Use* him. *Annihilate* him.'

'What are you all talking about?' Amanda's mum said, looking from one to another.

'Oh, nothing, nothing,' Mr Bunting lied, voice light and bright, eyes sparkling.

'No. Something's going on. I want to know what it is, or I'm going to call security.'

'Mum, he's—' Amanda choked on her words. The snake at her neck had suddenly constricted its coils, strangling her. But, even as she struggled in panic, Amanda knew all her mum could see was her daughter gasping for air.

'Amanda,' her mum cried, trying to get Amanda to sit up with one hand, trying to loosen her pyjamas with the other. 'Oh, Amanda! Amanda?' She turned to Mr Bunting. 'You. I don't care *why* you're here. Go get help. Quick. Can't you see she's choking?'

'Now they're busy,' Mr Bunting said, ignoring Mrs Shuffleup and turning back to Rudger, 'we can go back to *our* business, yes? Where were we?'

He began the gruesome chittering task of unhooking his jaw again.

Rudger wasn't watching. He was looking at Amanda and her mum. He could see the snake throttling her, but Mrs Shuffleup couldn't.

Could Mr Bunting's imaginary snakes *really* hurt Amanda? Could they *actually* strangle her? Rudger didn't know. But he had the feeling, the sense, the certainty that if only Amanda's mum could see them, then she'd be able to fight them, to pull them off, to free Amanda.

And although she couldn't see them *now*, although she was a grownup and grownups didn't have the sort of imagination to see all this stuff, he knew that once she had. He'd met Fridge, hadn't he? He knew Amanda's mum's old imaginary friend. And that meant that once upon a time she had been part of this world.

Mr Bunting had his imaginary-eating mouth open now. Rudger could feel the world beginning to tip up again.

'Amanda,' he shouted desperately. 'Amanda, tell your mum about Fridge. Tell her I met him. Tell her he's waiting for her. Tell her he'd come if she asked. Tell her about the mirror.'

'Mum,' Amanda wheezed.

'Hush, baby,' her mum said. 'Don't try to talk.'

'It's Rudger,' Amanda managed. 'He wants me to tell you…'

'What, darling?'

'About…about a fridge? I don't under—'

'What about the fridge, darling?'

Amanda paused as if she were listening to something far off. Her breaths whistled in her throat, and there were tears on her cheeks.

Her mum stroked her hand, kissed her brow.

'A dog?' Amanda whispered, finding each word hard to say, her breaths coming so short. 'Fridge…a dog? Rudger… Rudger met him.'

Amanda's mum looked at her, shocked.

'What?' she stuttered.

'He says,' Amanda could hardly get the words out, 'he's waiting. Use the…the mirror.'

It had taken Lizzie Downbeat ages before she'd realised Fridge wasn't a real dog. Even when he had talked to her from underneath the bed at night, she just thought her parents had found her the best dog in the world. She didn't know any better. It had only dawned slowly that no one else could see Fridge, that no one else seemed to know about him, that her parents denied having bought him for her. It was only then that she had realised what he was.

Imaginary.

Such a strange thing.

And now, here in this hospital room, where she'd spent so long hoping and wishing and, yes, *imagining* that her Amanda would wake up, here where her daughter finally *had* woken up (she wasn't imagining *that*, was she?), she thought she could smell Fridge's damp fur once again.

And, looking down at her daughter, she saw something else.

Not just sheets, not just her girl, but there was something else there.

She couldn't make it out. No sooner had she seen the something than it had gone again.

She heard a faint voice, a faint boy's voice from far away, saying, 'The mirror. Tell her about the mirror.'

Was it talking to her? It had sounded like mist speaking, it was so faint, so thin, but she looked around.

She saw the wardrobe where Amanda's clothes were hanging. The door was open and on the inside of the door was a full-length mirror.

She looked straight into it and saw herself reflected back. She looked tired, like she'd not slept for days. She felt it too. She'd not left Amanda's bedside for more than a few minutes this whole time. And there, next to her in the mirror, was Amanda in her bed with her wriggling green duvet.

No. That wasn't what it was. It wasn't a duvet, it was…

She looked down at the bed next to her and saw the snakes. They looked as real as anything and were coiling around and across her daughter, holding her tight, pinning her down.

'Snakes,' she said to herself. 'Why did it have to be snakes?'

She hated them. The way they coiled, the way they moved, magically sliding with hardly an effort, as if it was their sheer malevolent will that carried them forward. Even Oven ran when she found a slow worm in the garden, and that's not even a real snake, just a legless lizard.

199

This was mad. This was unreal, bizarre. But she didn't panic, she wouldn't panic, no matter how much she wanted to.

If snakes were what was pinning her daughter down, she thought, if snakes were the thing that was keeping her daughter from her arms, then she would deal with them. It was as simple as that. And then she smelt Fridge again, far off, somewhere way beyond the room, but the smell tickled at the back of her brain, and the familiar scent of his damp shaggy fur was enough to calm her.

Unafraid, she wrapped her fingers round the thick python curled around Amanda's neck, carefully uncoiling it. It was strong and fought against her and she could only move it slowly, but soon she'd created enough space for Amanda to take her first deep gulps of fresh air.

She heard the boy's voice again. She looked round and saw him, saw Rudger, for the very first time. She recognised him, as if she'd seen him before, though she knew she hadn't. He was familiar, a friend and he was struggling desperately, wriggling and grimacing in the grip of something she couldn't quite make out. It was a dark cloud, a shadow without shape, something dreadful, something, she had a clear feeling, even worse than snakes.

The boy caught her eye and the panic in his face subsided for a moment when he saw she was looking at him.

'Fridge remembers you,' he shouted. 'He called you his Lizzie. I think he's waiting.'

And as she watched, the shadow around him stepped back and the boy staggered towards the man in the Hawaiian shirt. He had his back to the bed now, hunched over and she knew something was wrong.

Rudger stretched out, began to drip in drops towards the bald man's mouth. It was as if she were watching a waterfall running in slow motion upwards into a sewer pipe.

She didn't know what to do.

'Help him, Mum,' Amanda said pleadingly behind her. 'Help him.'

Fridge woke up.

It was lunchtime in the library. There were real people milling about all over the place, but it wasn't their noise that had woken him. That hadn't been it. It hadn't been the beeping of the machine that checked the books out or the rattle of the automatic doors either. He was used to all that. It was something else.

He looked up at the notice board.

He'd been looking at it for years. Sometimes he'd gone off and had adventures, but recently he'd just stared. He was tired. He was old. He was frayed round the edges and Fading bit by bit.

One last job, he'd told himself. One last job and that would be it.

He looked up.

And he saw a picture that shouldn't have been there. A picture that *couldn't* have been there. In all his time he'd never seen a face

201

like that up there. Never. But the photos that appeared had always been of kids who needed a Friend, for one reason or another, and this photo was, really, no different. It was what he'd been waiting for. He'd known if he waited long enough it would come.

Fridge snatched the picture in his mouth and ran for the Corridor, lined with its forget-me-not wallpaper, in great loping lolloping wheezy strides.

Amanda half-sat up, half-lay on the bed. She was getting her breath back from the throttling snake, and, although she could breathe freely again for the moment, her hands and legs were still trapped.

But Amanda didn't care about the snakes. She was watching Rudger and Mr Bunting. She hadn't seen it before, hadn't seen the open mouth, the slurping up of an imaginary. In the car park she'd interrupted him, coming at him from behind. This was what she'd stopped then.

There was no way she could stop it now.

The fight with the serpents had drained her of so much strength. She was exhausted and on the edge of passing out. She couldn't imagine how to save Rudger this time.

'Help him, Mum,' she gasped, tears stinging her angry eyes. 'Help him.'

Rudger was stretching further and further. Beside him the girl watched, a step back, out of the way, a thin, pale, sad half-smile on her face.

And then, just as she thought he was gone, just as Mr Bunting had leant back and begun sucking harder than ever, just as Rudger began to elongate beyond endurance, to stretch out to infinity, with little blobs of him breaking off and falling up the fiend's throat, something happened.

Her mum stood up, walked over to Mr Bunting and said, 'Stop it. Leave him alone. I want you to leave the boy alone. He's with us. He's our Friend. You can't have him.'

Amanda was so proud of her. She loved her.

Mr Bunting was less impressed. Without turning around he flung his arm out and pushed her mum away.

She stumbled, slipped, fell back on to the bed and as she did so, as she swore and grabbed hold of the metal bedstead to stop herself from falling further, from out of the wardrobe burst the most unlikely thing.

A big black and white dog came running from nowhere, its tail wagging and its tongue lolling from the side of its mouth.

'Lizzie?' it barked. 'Lizzie?'

And, without looking where it was going, it banged into the back of Mr Bunting's girl, and sent her flying.

She in turn banged into Rudger, knocking him out of the way of Mr Bunting's voracious mouth.

Rudger snapped, like a stretched elastic band let go, back into the shape of a boy. He rolled across the floor and shuddered with relief.

('Lizzie, is that you?' barked the dog.)

The girl, on the other hand, staggered into the exact space where Rudger had been. Mr Bunting, in the middle of feasting, didn't seem to notice the interruption. He kept on sucking.

('Lizzie. My Lizzie,' the dog said, running to Amanda's mother.)

Amanda watched in horror. The girl stretched out, stretched thin, and screamed with a high wailing screeching hiss like the kettle at Granny Downbeat's house, but from far away, from some far great distance.

205

('Oh, Lizzie, there you are!' snuffled the dog at the foot of the bed, burying his head in Amanda's mum's arms.)

And in a moment the girl was gone. Vanished.

Mr Bunting had his eyes shut. This was his favourite moment of all. He savoured the feeding, the flavour, the taste of the imaginaries as he swallowed. They wriggled as they went down. Their fear and panic added spice. It made him feel whole, complete, satisfied.

He relished the moment. It was exquisite, like a liquid jewel sliding down his throat.

And then it was over.

He'd swallowed the boy in one last quick slurp, but…

…but something wasn't right.

The boy tasted rank, tasted rotten. Like old meat left out on the countertop too long. Like bread six months in the bread bin. Like dust.

But he'd looked so tasty, had smelt so good…

Rudger had been knocked to the floor as something banged into him from behind, and he'd rolled away, free from Mr Bunting's hunger.

He looked back from where he landed and with a gasp of shock and surprise saw the girl vanish up into Mr Bunting's gullet, swirling round like dirty dishwater down a plughole and then, with a sickly *pop*, she was gone.

Somewhere Rudger smelt damp dog.

Mr Bunting clutched at his throat. His mouth snapped shut, his moustache settled back in place. He coughed as if he had a fishbone caught. His eyes bulged. He coughed again. Banged on his ribcage.

Rudger watched, fear, worry and hope beating inside his heart, unevenly.

'Uh,' Mr Bunting said, a hand on his chest. 'Uh, uh, uh,' as if it were a sentence that meant something. And then he began to shrivel.

Mr Bunting, a big man with a shining bald head and bright clothes, began to shrink. His skin grew saggy and baggy and wrinkled with lines, blemished with spots. His moustache thinned and grew grey, then white. He got shorter, his nails cracked, his knees buckled, he bent over. He wheezed, he coughed. His eyes dimmed, grew misty. His skin grew grey and blotchy. Cobwebs spread across the dark glasses perched on his now pockmarked forehead. Even his gaily patterned Hawaiian shirt dimmed, dulled, grew patchy and threadbare.

Rudger remembered the stories he'd heard at the campfire and made his own guess as to what had happened. All the years Mr Bunting had stolen, the extra year of life he'd been granted each time he ate an imaginary, now that he had eaten *his own* imaginary, well, it was all catching up with him, centuries of it. He was becoming old, becoming his true age.

Mr Bunting opened his eyes. He looked around the hospital room. It was dimmer than he remembered. It was growing dark.

He knew what he'd eaten. Knew who he'd eaten.

He coughed, hacked, chokingly.

'Where are you, boy?' he gasped, looking round for Rudger. If he could just eat one more time, he thought, he'd feel better. 'Where are you?' But he couldn't see the wretched boy anywhere.

There was just the girl in her bed and her mother kneeling on the floor in front of it.

The boy (Roger, was it?) had vanished.

Rudger shuddered as Mr Bunting looked straight at him.

'Uh, uh, uh, uh,' the old man said, before looking away.

He didn't see Rudger. Couldn't see him any more.

Rudger breathed a sigh of relief.

The hunger was awful. It felt like his insides were hollow, like he was nothing but a great empty hole.

Swallowing her had destroyed him. They'd been together so long, she was a part of him and he was a part of her. Would he live without her? *Could* he live without her? He didn't know.

He couldn't recall the exact terms of the bargain he'd made. It had all been so long ago.

All he knew was the hunger.

Just as the imaginaries needed to be believed in to go on, so he needed to eat that belief to keep himself going. He had lived so far beyond the ordinary lifetime that it was the only thing that sustained him any more. Oh, he liked the taste of a nice cup of tea, Earl Grey if you'd be so kind, but it passed straight through him. It was only the slick slippery slither of fresh imaginary that filled him up.

But eating *her* had been like eating his own hand. Once you start you find you're chewing on your wrist, and then your arm, and then your shoulder, and soon enough you've eaten yourself, and then in a final gulp you've vanished down your own throat. That was what it felt like.

The hunger was aching in him, burning. That and the loneliness. Everything he cared for, every*one* he cared for, everything he'd known was all long gone. And she had been the very last of it.

But he couldn't even remember her name.

That struck him as odd.

And then he couldn't remember. Couldn't remember. Couldn't remember.

FOURTEEN

The snakes had gone. When Mr Bunting had shrivelled and his girl had vanished, the snakes had just turned to smoke. The room smelt strange, gunpowdery and acrid, but at least, at last, it was over.

'Excuse me,' Amanda's mum said, poking her head out of the door. 'Is there a nurse about?'

She'd taken charge in the way the best adults do.

Fridge was sitting at the foot of the bed watching her with huge damp eyes. She'd helped Rudger to his feet, sat him in the chair beside the bed. As far as she could tell he wasn't badly hurt by all the fighting and all the other stuff that had been going on.

That had been odd, holding the arm of this boy she'd heard so much about, had shared a house with, but had never met before.

She hadn't blinked though (there would be a time for wondering about all this later on). She had just helped him up and edged him towards the bed.

She had sat him down with Amanda and had looked at the shrivelled Mr Bunting. Something needed to be done about him. He was muttering, half-deaf, half-blind. A poor old man who was powerless, forgetful and, it seemed, at last, quite harmless.

When the nurse came Mrs Shuffleup just pointed at him.

'I think he's lost,' she explained. 'He doesn't seem to know where he is.'

'Oh dear, love,' the nurse said. She turned to Mr Bunting. 'What's your name, love?' She almost shouted the words, but kindly.

'Uh?' said Mr Bunting.

'Oh, come on then. Come with me, we'll see if we can't find out where you're meant to be. Get you back to bed, find you a cup of tea, eh? My name's Joan, love. You lean on me arm. Come on.'

'Joan,' said Mr Bunting in a gasp, his eyes brightening. 'Yes, that's…uh…that's it.'

'That's what, love?' asked the nurse.

Mr Bunting looked at her blankly. Dimness had sunk across his face again.

'Uh?'

'Oh dear,' said the nurse. 'You forgotten? Come on, love. It'll all be okay. Someone's probably looking for you, aren't they?'

The nurse led Mr Bunting out of the room. He took small shuffling steps and held onto her arm.

When they were half out the door she turned to Amanda's mum and said, 'I'm sorry about this, love. Poor old chap. It's easy to get confused sometimes, you take a wrong turn and all these corridors look the same. I hope he wasn't a bother. You two okay, really?'

Mrs Shuffleup looked around the room, smiled and said, 'Yeah, I think we're all fine. Thank you for your help.'

A week later Amanda was fit enough to go home.

She sat in the back of the car with Rudger.

'Oh, Lizzie,' Fridge said, half his words getting carried away on the wind, 'when did you learn to drive?'

'Get your head in the car, Fridge,' Amanda's mum said, laughing.

'How come he gets to sit in the front seat?' asked Amanda, with only the slightest annoyance in her voice. 'I'm the one with the broken arm. Shouldn't I get the special treatment?'

'Darling,' her mum said over her shoulder. 'Fridge hasn't been in a car before. He was a big coward when I was a little girl. He spent most of his time under the bed. He didn't like the noise of the engine.'

'It's not that,' Fridge said. 'I just used to get carsick.'

'Uh oh,' said Rudger.

'I'm all right now,' the dog barked. 'Now that Lizzie's all grown up.'

'Do you remember,' Mrs Shuffleup asked, 'when we went on holiday? We went to Lyme Regis. We went fossilling and you found that bone the chef in the hotel had "lost" from the kitchen? You told me it was a dinosaur bone. It was only three days later, when Mum wondered what the smell was and looked under the bed, that I found out what it really was—'

'Hang on,' Amanda said, interrupting with a finger in the air. (She'd been thinking.) 'If Fridge wouldn't go in the car, how did he go on holiday with you?'

'I just met them there,' Fridge replied. 'It was easier that way.'

'I met a dinosaur,' Rudger said nonchalantly. 'It was a *Tyrannosaurus rex* called Snowflake.'

'Ooh,' barked Fridge. 'Me too. Me too.'

Grownups aren't meant to see everything, not always, not forever, and a few weeks later Amanda's mum missed Rudger at the breakfast table.

'Is Rudger coming down, Amanda?'

213

'He's sat right there, Mum,' Amanda said.

'Oh.' She felt embarrassed. 'I'm sorry, Rudger,' she said to a patch of empty air exactly where Rudger wasn't sitting.

Fridge, who was half-asleep by the back door, looked up and said, 'Lizzie, don't worry yourself. He's Amanda's Friend. You're not really meant to see him at all. Look, I'm still here.' He wagged his tail.

'But even you look a bit thin, Fridge,' she said.

'I'm just tired,' the dog replied.

School had begun again. Amanda had missed the first week and a bit, but the day came when even she thought she was well enough to return.

Amanda and her mum bumped into Julia Radiche and her mother at the school gates.

The two girls smiled politely and walked into school together.

'Does Amanda still have that imaginary friend, Mrs Shuffleup?' Julia's mum asked.

'What, Rudger?'

'Yes that's right.'

'How did you know about Rudger?' Mrs Shuffleup asked. She wasn't going to let on that he'd told them all about his adventures in the Radiche household.

'My Julia mentioned him.' Mrs Radiche lowered her voice and looked around to make sure she wasn't overheard before going on. 'She had a funny turn during the holidays. Thought she had an imaginary friend too.'

'Oh, that's nice,' Amanda's mum said, ruffling Fridge's head. 'I think they're—'

'It was just awful, Mrs Shuffleup,' Julia's mum said, ignoring her. 'I was dreadfully worried. She was acting so oddly. It's not natural. I took her to see Dr Peterson at the hospital. He's a specialist, a child psychologist.' She half-whispered, half-mouthed the last two words, as if embarrassed by them. 'He came highly recommended.'

'You took Julia to a child psychologist?' Amanda's mum asked loudly.

'Yes,' Mrs Radiche said, looking around guiltily. 'And it was brilliant. The moment we got there, she was cured. Not a single hallucination from that day to this. Cured.'

'How dreadful.'

'I can give you his phone number if you like?'

'I don't think so,' Amanda's mum said. 'I think Amanda's doing fine.'

'Hmm,' said Julia's mum.

'Did she ask after me?' Rudger asked that evening.

'No, not a word,' Amanda said.

It was dark in the bedroom. Amanda was in bed, Rudger was in his wardrobe. Everything was back the way it had been before.

'Did you ask her?'

'About Veronica?'

'Yeah.'

'Well, I did mention the name a *few* times, just accidentally in passing. You know, "Will you pass me the pencil sharpener, Veronica?" and "Can I sit next to you for lunch, Veronica?" Stuff like that.'

'And what did she say?'

'"My name's not Veronica," and "Leave me alone, you weirdo." That sort of thing.'

'I'm sorry.'

'Don't be silly, Rudger. I don't care 'bout that. It was very funny. She's a weird one, Julia, but I like her. And I promise I'll stop doing it tomorrow.' She thought for a moment. 'Or the day after.'

The next morning Rudger was sat in the front room with Fridge looking out of the window, watching the cat.

Sometimes Oven, Amanda's cat, behaved as if she had seen Rudger (although no one was ever really sure), but they all agreed that she never saw Fridge. The dog would lie down beside her where she was sleeping and she would slowly be pushed off the sofa or down the stairs, but, in her cattish way, she would just yawn, stretch, wash her ear and wander off to sleep somewhere else.

'That's not Oven,' Rudger said, all of a sudden.

'No,' said Fridge.

The cat that was sat on the front lawn, washing its leg, was definitely not Oven. Rudger recognised the mangled outline, the torn ear, the odd eyes, the bent tail.

'It's Zinzan,' he said.

Rudger ran to the front door, pulled it open.

'Hey, Zinzan,' he called.

'Rudger,' said the cat, strolling past him and into the house.

Fridge was in the hallway. He was lurking in the shadows.

'No,' he said in a gruff bark.

The cat hopped up onto the bottom step of the stairs and scratched its ear.

It blinked slowly. Said nothing.

Fridge shrank back further into the shadows.

'Not this time,' he said. 'Not any more.'

Zinzan said nothing.

There was a tinkling bell upstairs.

Oven appeared on the very top step. Stopped. Saw Zinzan. Turned tail and ran back to hide in someone's bedroom.

Zinzan laughed a cattish laugh.

'You don't want to come with me?'

'No,' said Fridge.

'You know what that means.'

Fridge nodded.

'What's going on?' asked Rudger, thinking he understood, but sort of hoping he didn't.

'Fridge?' called Amanda's mum from the kitchen. 'Can you smell something?'

'Lizzie?'

'Ah, there you are,' she said, coming into the hallway and stroking his shaggy fur. 'There's a weird smell coming from somewhere. Can you—'

She saw the strange cat on the bottom step.

It blinked at her. Slowly.

'How did *you* get in here? Oven!' she called up the stairs. 'Someone's in your territory.' Then she spoke to Zinzan. 'Shoo, go on you, get out. Awful smelly cat—'

'It's alright, Lizzie,' Fridge said. 'It's with me.'

'You mean it's a…?'

'No. It's a cat. Just a cat I know. It'll be gone in a minute.'

When Amanda came home from school, she ran inside.

Rudger told her the news.

Fridge had gone.

He was old, Rudger explained. He went down the end of the garden after lunch and the wind took him.

Rudger had sat with the dog. He'd liked Fridge. But now, a few hours later, he already found it difficult to remember exactly what the dog had looked like. He was forgetting, just like he'd forgotten… Oh, he thought, he'd forgotten someone. Who was it?

218

After Fridge had blown away, Rudger had come back inside and looked at the photographs around the house. He wasn't in any of them, except one that Amanda had pinned to the cork notice board in her bedroom. She'd drawn him in, in felt tip. She said it still counted.

Photographs are all we have of some people. Those and our memories.

Imagination is slippery, Rudger knew that well enough. Memory doesn't hold it tight, it has trouble enough holding on to the real, remembering the real people who are lost.

He was pleased she had the photo, that she'd made the photo, that she had something of him that wouldn't fade, because one day, he knew, as unlikely as it seemed, she would forget him. It was what happened in time, no one's fault, just the way things go. But years from now, as a grownup, she'd find the photo tucked away in a drawer, or hidden between the pages of a book, and look at it with its odd addition. Maybe something of Rudger would slip back into her mind, or maybe she'd just shake her head and laugh at her over-enthusiastic youthful penmanship (or at her haircut), but either way...well, either way would be enough for Rudger.

'I'm sorry, Mum,' Amanda said that afternoon.

'What's that, love?'

'About Fridge.'

'What about the fridge?'

'No, about...' Amanda stopped talking. Grownups weren't made to see everything, someone had told her that. They forgot things so easily sometimes. She looked at Rudger.

'I'm never going to forget you,' she said, and she meant it.

'What's that?' her mum said.

'I was talking to Rudger.'

'Oh, Rudger. Is he still around?'

'Come on,' said Amanda, and she and Rudger went out of the back door into the garden.

'Dinner's in twenty minutes,' her mum called.

The two of them ran in the sunshine, the grass under their bare feet.

Rudger was the first into the den, crawling under the thorn bush.

'What is it?' he asked, eagerly. 'What is it today?'

'Can't you tell?' Amanda said, wriggling in beside him, reaching up and flicking some switches. Lights whirred and engines hummed. 'Rudger, my friend, it's whatever you want it to be.'